PETER MINTO

MESSAGE FROM THE DEAD

Counter-terrorism and deceit amid the canals of Venice

MEREO
Cirencester

Mereo Books

1A The Wool Market Dyer Street Cirencester Gloucestershire GL7 2PR
An imprint of Memoirs Publishing www.mereobooks.com

Message from the Dead: 978-1-86151-824-8

First published in Great Britain in 2017
by Mereo Books, an imprint of Memoirs Publishing

A CIP catalogue record for this book is available from the British Library.

Cover design and artwork - Ray Lipscombe

The address for Memoirs Publishing Group Limited can be found at www.memoirspublishing.com

The Memoirs Publishing Group Ltd Reg. No. 7834348

The Memoirs Publishing Group supports both The Forest Stewardship Council® (FSC®) and the PEFC® leading international forest-certification organisations. Our books carrying both the FSC label and the PEFC® and are printed on FSC®-certified paper. FSC® is the only forest-certification scheme supported by the leading environmental organisations including Greenpeace. Our paper procurement policy can be found at www.memoirspublishing.com/environment

Typeset in 12/18pt Century Schoolbook
by Wiltshire Associates Publisher Services Ltd. Printed and bound in Great Britain
by Marston Book Services Ltd, Oxfordshire

Printed on FSC approved paper

To Christine (Kit)

AUTHOR'S NOTE:

The bars I have referred to in Venice are real and most welcoming, and Andrea and his Ristorante Tre Archi has been a favourite of mine for over twelve years. Also Anarchy beer is a real 'real' ale, brewed in Morpeth, Northumberland. And Barry Langroyd Hanson is a talented Bradford artist.

CHAPTER 1

April 17th 2010
Marlow, Buckinghamshire, England

The house where they met was a fine late Edwardian building situated in a quiet, tree-lined street that sloped gently down towards the Thames. Like the others in the street it was detached, and its privacy was ensured by a high stone wall and an equally high solid wooden gate which, when the house was occupied, could only be operated remotely from inside the grounds.

There were no expensive cars parked outside any of the houses, but the area had an unmistakable aura of affluence. The house, named The Lilacs, was one of several properties in the area that was occasionally, but not regularly, used by Brian Polliter, the overall head of Britain's anti-terrorist and intelligence-gathering organisation. Today a meeting had been called there, at very short notice. There were only four people present: Polliter, who had called the meeting, and the three men who had responsibility for covert operations in three of the European sectors, Northern, Southern and Eastern. Of these three Derek Agnew was the senior, so if there was any overlap between his Southern sector and the others he had the authority to override the other two. But although Polliter had the utmost confidence in all three of them and, as a result, allowed them a great deal of freedom in the way they ran their teams, there were occasions when he demanded that they all, including Agnew, follow his directive.

"Gentlemen, I apologise if any of you have been inconvenienced by my bringing you together at such short notice, but as you well know, events do not always occur at times of our choosing," Polliter began.

There was a quiet murmur of agreement. Polliter pulled his chair to one side of the front of the table where the others were already seated. "You will have noticed that Gordon of the Western sector has not been able to join us. As I'm sure you know his health is not good, and the person who will replace him has been delayed by weather problems in North Africa. The urgency of what I am going to say to you today couldn't be delayed by vagaries in the weather, but when he arrives in the UK I'll bring him up to date."

Polliter noted the raised eyebrows of the other three and continued, "It's a departure from our normal practice of promotion from within, but he has proved himself and I think he could be a particularly useful link with your Southern sector." He nodded towards Agnew. "But you'll be the judge of that," he added hurriedly.

He then turned to the projector standing on the table and a large screen on the front wall. "If you wouldn't mind, Stannard, drawing those blinds for me?" He switched the projector on. "As you will see, I have made a random choice of six major European newspapers. I know you will be familiar with them and indeed many others, but as I will be using this in a presentation to my political masters later in the week, they are included here."

There then followed six mastheads, those of *The Guardian, La Repubblica, Le Monde, El Mundo, Het Nieuwsbled* and *De Telegraaf*. The rest of his slide show took no more than a few minutes. It consisted of images taken from the front pages of each of the newspapers. The dates varied, although all were in the last six months, but the main headlines and the accompanying photographs were all concerned with terrorist attacks in major cities in each of the countries.

Polliter switched off the projector and Stannard, unasked, opened the blinds.

"That wasn't meant to be an eye-opener for any of you," said Polliter rather apologetically. "I would be the last person to try to tell you that Europe – the old Europe as we knew it – is in turmoil, in crisis. The seeds of it have been around for far longer than any of the politicians are prepared to admit. However, recent events in Turkey, the Netherlands, France, Belgium and Germany have caused them to reassess the situation and this has resulted in a general consensus that something needs to be done. Belatedly, talks are being held, but I'm afraid too much of their thinking is based on outdated scenarios. Consequently they are working to a time scale which they measure in decades. The problems of today, next week, or even next year are being ignored or are considered by some to be insoluble. And it is in that vacuum of indecision or despair that terrorism flourishes and our greatest threats lie."

He paused, looked at each of them in turn and then, with a mannerism they all knew well, he raked his top teeth over his bottom lip – a clear indication to them that he was far from happy with what he was about to say next. If they had not been fully attentive before, they were now.

He continued, "However, as there is no one enemy to be confronted, then consequently there is no single solution. Our main role, as ever, is intelligence gathering, but, and this is the main reason for calling you here today, the situation is now so unpredictable and fast-moving that direct action may have to be taken by you or your operatives without my obtaining the necessary clearance and passing that on to you. I fear that the possibility of this becomes greater every day. I'm sure you all remember the great furore in the British press several years ago when armed members of the security service were accused of operating a shoot-to-kill policy. I don't want to go over that ground again other than to state that the security of our people is paramount. Unfortunately, and not of our doing, the conditions under which we operate to achieve that have changed radically in recent years."

Again he paused, gazing out of the leaded window at a sky which seemed to be growing darker as he spoke. The three men waited.

He turned his attention back to them and continued, "In practical terms, this means that if you deem it to be necessary, then the chain of command, and with it the responsibility, ends with you. Believe me when I say that I am not ducking issues here but simply and hopefully allowing you the freedom to do what you believe is necessary for the safety of our country and its people. I am not overstating the case when I say the situation is becoming critical."

He paused again, once more raking his teeth over his lip, obviously unhappy with what he had to ask of them, before continuing. "However, this is not something that I can impose upon you. So if any of you are not prepared to take on this greater role, please say so now."

Polliter waited a moment. There being no response, he nodded.

"As I expected. So, for us to be singing from the same hymn sheet, I have identified two main areas of concern. Next year there may be more, but as you know we deal with the present and we'll leave the politicians to talk and argue about the future.

"So we start with illegal immigration into Europe from North Africa, the Middle East, etcetera, which is reaching almost epidemic proportions. That in itself is causing major problems for the receiving countries and in some areas we have seen an upsurge in ethnic violence. Of the various routes being used, the one through Greece and the Adriatic countries and the one into Southern Italy are probably causing the greatest concern. Taking advantage of all of this are various terrorist organizations which are infiltrating members into the vast numbers of these immigrants as well as among genuine asylum seekers. The primary purpose of these groups appears to be to overthrow Western culture by violent means. There are many of them, but perhaps the principal ones at the moment are Al Qaida, Boko Haram and Isis, although there are also a number of small but dangerous splinter groups. As well as perpetrating terrorist acts, they are seeking to gain maximum publicity for their actions which, they seem to believe, will bring them more adherents to their ranks. Where their next target will be is difficult to determine but, as we have recently seen, Europe is certainly in their sights.

"Pulling these points together, I see the Northern Adriatic from Slovenia round to Austria and into Northern Italy as the most likely. But, and it is a big but, no areas can consider themselves completely safe. We live in difficult and dangerous times, gentlemen, and the recent events in Paris and Brussels are a timely reminder to us."

He stopped speaking, leaned back in his chair and for several minutes stared up at the ceiling before he continued.

"I'm sure you are all aware of much of what I've said in trying to identify the general problems, and in your own particular areas you know the specifics. However, although I came to sound you out about the widening of your responsibility, even as I was travelling here this morning I received a worrying report from the office of the Italian Anti-Terrorist Commission. Two days ago they foiled a planned terrorist attack in Rome and from information gathered they believe there are group members who are aiming in some way to widen their target areas. The USA seems to have been suggested, and it is being taken very seriously by Washington. It has also been seriously suggested that there is the possibility they may be changing their tactics from mass killings to more specific targets."

He dropped his chin onto his chest and spoke again, very quietly. “I feel very much as I think a fellow Scotsman must have felt hundreds of years ago. Robert the Bruce, watching a spider making repeated attempts to climb a wall. ‘Try, try and try again’. You know the tale, I’m sure. That is the situation we are in, you three in particular. You have men and women in perilous situations attempting to obtain information that could enable the Western world to overcome this urban guerrilla threat. It’s a situation that is more serious than any we’ve had to face in the last thirty years. Our embassy staffs are still functioning, but politics can restrict them. More and more we are going to rely on information gatherers; our own, your teams and those of our allies. And, as I said earlier, where the threat is imminent, action must ignore the niceties of protocol. All I can say at this juncture is that amongst the powers that be I will back you to the hilt and do my damnedest to ensure you have the means to achieve the near impossible. But achieve it you must. Good luck.”

He rose and formally shook hands with the three of them. Then, as he made to leave the room, as if in an attempt to lighten the tone, he turned and suggested, “If you’re intending to stay in town for lunch I can thoroughly recommend the Two Brewers pub and restaurant down by the river barely fifty yards from here. Can’t join you I’m afraid, my political masters desire to be kept in the picture.” With that he quietly closed the door.

Agnew and his two colleagues sat back, looked at each other, and once more raised their eyebrows. Agnew broke the silence.

"He was always one for fine food," he said. "I suggest we take his advice and give the Two Brewers some custom."

CHAPTER 2

14th May, 2011

Steve Cromarty, one of Agnew's most experienced operatives, was doing what he hated most – kicking his heels in a transit camp, this time in the former Jugoslavia. To make it worse, when the call had come for him to carry out a reconnaissance survey of the borders of Ceuta and Melilla, Spain's two enclaves on the north coast of Africa, he had been just one month into a well-earned leave period in the 'safe house' Agnew had allocated to him. As with all leaves there was an 'on call' element, but Steve had hoped there wouldn't be too much of that as the apartment was very much to his liking, as was the area where it was situated in north-east England. And if he was perfectly honest, Katherine, the part-time librarian whom Agnew had laid on to help him in his research at the library of the Literary and Philosophical Society in Newcastle, was proving to be a very pleasant bonus.

The research was intended to give some sort of validity to Steve's weekday role without putting him in a rigid time frame. Agnew, the organiser par excellence, had even chosen the subject of the research: 'Possible links between the port of Newcastle and the Hanseatic League ports of the Baltic area in the late seventeenth century'. The usefulness of that topic meant Steve could use it as 'necessary research abroad' to explain any absences. However, to have made up some sort of spurious excuse to get out of it would have been pointless, especially when he'd been told that the job would take him no more than two weeks.

The completion date was correct, but what hadn't been factored in was a transport delay. The RAF plane which was supposed to be carrying him back to Britain had developed a mechanical fault which had caused it to divert to the airstrip at this transit camp. A two-day delay while repairs were carried out had lengthened into four, thanks to several severe thunderstorms in the area. Then, the previous evening, the conditions had improved and it was decided take-off would be at six the next morning. As a result, Steve was in the canteen at four-thirty that morning.

There was only one other person breakfasting at that ungodly hour. They nodded to each other and sat at the same table. Neither of them spoke for several minutes; drinking mugs containing a coffee concoction and gnawing through cheese rolls seemed to require all their attention. Then the other man, who was shorter and older than Steve, broke the silence.

"I'm Maurice Dempsey."

"Yeah, I know," muttered Steve.

Dempsey, not put off by the lack of enthusiasm, continued, "Are you for home or are you active?"

"I'm on a flight when I've finished this, which I have." Steve pushed himself to his feet. "Good to have met you again. We can continue this conversation some other time."

As he strode out of the canteen Steve wondered why he'd been so curt with Dempsey. They'd only met once before, about eight years ago, on a training course in the wilds of Knoydart, north-west Scotland. There had been twelve of them, all Agnew's men. Physically and mentally they'd had to work their bollocks off, so there had been little time, energy or inclination for much in the way of socialising. What little there was hadn't seemed to involve Dempsey very much; he was older than the rest and his background was very different, especially from Steve's. He was, or had been, an academic who spoke several languages fluently. Steve, at that time, had formed the opinion that he considered himself to be rather superior. However, the passage of time, along with snippets of information about him that had filtered down to Steve, had caused him to modify his view. Why he had made no attempt to have a reasonable conversation with him that morning he did not know; he could only put it down to his impatience with the delay in his own travel. Although he doubted if they would ever be close friends, he vowed to make more of an effort if their paths should happen to cross again.

Three quarters of an hour after Steve had left him alone to finish his breakfast, Dempsey and two Kosovans climbed into an armoured vehicle to begin a journey north. With them a case of gold coins, the region's all-purpose lubricant and due to be delivered to an anti-government group, had already been loaded; bribes and the procurement of weapons could only be successfully achieved with the backing of gold. The journey was high priority. Very few were aware of the gold consignment and its supposed destination; even fewer knew the real reason for the journey.

Steve, having nothing better to do to fill in his time before his flight, had watched their departure from the compound. Their route took them into the foothills of the Mokra Gora, a mile or so beyond the camp, and then the vehicle was out of sight, only a dust cloud indicating where they had passed. By then Steve had lost interest.

Thirty-five minutes after they had left, a heavy explosion echoed around the hills. In the compound the reaction was rapid and well-practised; two vehicles with troops and medics on board were on their way almost immediately.

"That road's been clear for more than six months," said a young squaddie.

"Not any longer," answered his mate.

Apart from that comment, although there were now more personnel moving around the camp, there was a noticeable lack of conversation. Steve made his way back into the canteen until he heard the first rescue crew returning, when he moved out into the gravelled compound. The young REME captain who had led the detail was obviously still coming to terms with what he had seen. As he passed Steve he seemed to welcome the opportunity to speak out, although it was a curt, clipped message.

"Not a roadside bomb, direct hit by a rocket. They hadn't

a chance. There's not much of them left to bring back."

Steve shrugged. "At least it was quick."

It was another hour before a second rescue team made it back to camp. They unloaded three body bags.

"We did the best we could, sir," Steve heard their officer say to the CO, "but we can't be exactly sure what we've got and in which bags. We did notice one strange thing though. It looked as if they'd stopped about half a mile from where they were hit and there was a trace of some lighter tracks."

"You think they had some sort of problem?"

"Who knows? They certainly had five minutes later, but the two may not be linked."

If there was any further conjecture, Steve left it at that. He didn't see any point in getting involved. It wasn't his affair. Regrettably, their conversation earlier that morning would never be continued. His thoughts turned to his flight back to England, which was due to take off in fifteen minutes.

Five days after his return to Britain, when he was again in West Monkseaton, Steve received a message from Agnew. In it he suggested that it would be fitting if he attended a service at Mountsett Crematorium, Gateshead, as Dempsey's family had in the past had some links with the area. Steve had heard it said that Agnew had a caring side, but he also knew that a suggestion from him could not just be about that.

On the day, he was one of a congregation of four – not much of a send-off, he thought. After that, apart from a couple of very short assignments and his annual health check, which included a five-day physical assessment at the old CCPR centre in North Wales, he had a lengthy spell when he was able to settle into his routine at the library and enjoy a growing friendship with Katherine.

CHAPTER 3

Venice, mid-May 2011

It was a dull, cool evening and Dempsey was tired. For five days he had been travelling north on a circuitous route from the eastern Adriatic, a route that had been carefully planned for him. The first leg had been the longest, the most worrying and the most uncomfortable – particularly the timing of his transfer from the vehicle carrying him from the transit camp until a few minutes before the rocket attack took place.

The Trabant that picked him up was manned by two men who hardly spoke during the journey north into Slovenia. The car was old and its engine and suspension struggled to cope with the poorly-maintained minor roads they used. Despite that, they reached the Slovenian border post with Italy at a few minutes after midnight on the 14th. Dempsey then left the car, and the men, and simply walked past the old concrete customs buildings. He was unchallenged by the guards, who were more interested in the groups of Italian men who were stocking up with cartons of cheap American cigarettes.

His next lift, to the outskirts of Trieste, was in a modern Alfa Romeo and he felt he was returning to a modern Western European state. After that the next four days involved public transport with the nights being spent in small, cheap hotels.

The final leg of his journey was the shortest, from Padua to Venice. At eighteen forty-five he boarded the normal service bus at the Piazzale Boschetti terminal. He had two large suitcases which he placed in the luggage area behind the driver and took a seat near the rear of the vehicle away from the other passengers. He was normally a sociable person, keen to keep up his fluency in many of the languages of the Adriatic area, but this evening he felt happier alone.

As the bus pulled out of the station, his mind suddenly flashed back twenty-five years to the time when he had come to the university there as a young graduate research student. Then he had been excited, eager and ready, with the confidence of youth, to take on the world. Now, worldly-wise, world-weary and cynical, he had a single objective – to disappear.

The journey was not the uneventful one that everyone had expected. Luck and the driver's quick reaction resulted in the bus narrowly avoiding a three-car collision on the causeway linking Venice to the mainland. But they were held up for more than an hour while traffic police made their enquiries and then organised breakdown vehicles to clear the way for them. By the time they pulled into the Piazzale Roma terminal in Venice, it was dusk and the other passengers were out of their seats. As soon as the bus stopped they were off, hurrying to catch one of the late evening *vaporetti* to take them into the main areas of the city.

Dempsey was the last to leave. He paused to have a word with the driver, who was patiently waiting for him as he pulled his cases after him.

"Well at least we got here safe and sound," he said.

"True. Some of those in that pile-up back there will never be the same again."

Dempsey nodded grimly and simply answered, "*Destino*."

As he started to make his way in the direction the other passengers had taken towards the roadway leading down to the Canal Grande, a young man approached him.

"Can I help you with those cases?" he said. "They seem very heavy."

"Bulky but not heavy," Dempsey replied. "In any case I've had greater burdens in the past."

"Your name isn't Atlas, is it?" This was the response he had been expecting.

"No. My shoulders aren't really big enough." He put down one of the cases and proffered his left hand, which the other shook enthusiastically.

"I began to seriously wonder if I'd been given the correct time of your arrival."

Dempsey explained the cause for the delay, then asked, "Is it far from here?"

"No more than twenty minutes' walk, four bridges."

They set off and, as they crossed the second bridge, the Ponte delle Guglie, and made their way along the Fondamenta di Cannareggio, Dempsey broke their silence.

"Do you live near here?"

"No. I live on the mainland, in Mestre."

"Well if my apartment's in this area I know it well from years back. You can give me its number and the key and you can make your way back to Mestre."

"I have my instructions," the young man replied. "My orders."

Dempsey understood and, without further discussion, allowed himself to be taken along narrow, near-deserted *calli*. They crossed the Ghetto area and then went beyond it. As his guide had said, two further bridges brought them to the apartment, which was located in the Calle delle Conterie.

The young man handed over the key. "I'll tell them you've arrived," he said.

Dempsey smiled. "Do that. And in your written report remember to spell my name correctly; it has a P in the middle. I'm very particular about that."

The young man looked puzzled, but nodded and left.

* * *

In the apartment, in a space under the bottom shelf of a heavily-carved wooden cabinet in the living room, Dempsey found his new passport, the address, the key to what was to be a more permanent location in the city, and sufficient euros to fund a reasonable lifestyle for several months. There was also three days' supply of food in the fridge.

Although he was more tired than hungry, he made himself a cold meat salad, then, opening both of his cases, he transferred everything into one and put the remains of the food into the other. He made a quick check to ensure he'd left no obvious trace of having been there. Now was the time to move on. There was no way he was going to stay there with that young man aware of his arrival.

He took both the cases with him. The calle was only dimly lit by two low-wattage lamps. He stood for a moment listening; there were no footsteps. Twenty yards from the apartment door there was a narrow opening to a small canal. He opened the lighter of the two cases and gently sank it into the dark waters.

* * *

Dempsey made his way back to the Fondamenta delle Cappuccine. He was familiar with the system of numbering of properties in the city and in years past he had spent some time in Cannareggio. He crossed the second bridge into the Campo del Ghetto Nuovo and, crossing one more bridge, he came to his new apartment in the Calle degli Ormesini. There was no food there but the water, electricity and gas were working, and inside the washing machine in the bathroom he found a small rucksack containing several items of clothing. A quick check confirmed that none of them were new but all were of his size. Moving back into the living room he looked more closely at his new passport; Pinot Cordon, age 48, place of birth Pecs, Hungary – that was near enough to his grandmother's family area. The photograph was recognisable. He was satisfied with it; he would have no problem filling in any details about the earlier life of Pinot Cordon if that was ever required. He then carefully cut up his Maurice Dempsey passport, used a gas ring to burn each page and then used a bowl and a spoon to crush the embers before flushing them down the toilet.

Tomorrow Pinot Cordon, now a resident of Venice, would begin to fashion a new life for himself. How soon Agnew would put in place his contact was out of his hands.

CHAPTER 4

During his first eight months in Venice, Dempsey, or rather Pinot, moved three times. As he explained to the *immobiliare*, after many years in business, which had involved much travelling in southern and eastern Europe, he was now looking forward to settling down and indulging his passions of writing and painting. He was prepared to rent for several months until he found the right property, and then he would buy. Although property prices in the city were high, he had indicated to her that money would not be a problem.

The apartment he had moved to after finding his new passport would have been very acceptable, but he knew it could only be temporary; as soon as Agnew had arranged his contact he knew he would be expected to move at least twice, using the services of one of the many estate agents. The only condition was that Agnew must be informed of his eventual final address. But that was in the future; in the meantime he had started to make sketches of canal scenes almost as soon as he'd settled in and in places where there were no other artists at work.

A week passed before a young man stood behind him and commented on his work.

"I thought I knew all the artists working in this area," he said in very good English with just a hint of an Italian accent.

"Whether I can sell any remains to be seen," Pinot replied without looking up.

The young man considered this, then nodded. "There is a lot of competition but if you tried to suggest a hint of Hockney in your work," he suggested.

Pinot looked up, leaned back on his stool, and smiled. "Or even that other artist bloke from Bradford. I forget his name, but he's got talent."

"Barry Langroyd," was the quick reply.

"That's him. B L Hanson," answered Pinot and then he returned his attention to his work.

The young man nodded and walked on. The brief conversation satisfied them both.

Two days later Pinot was at the same canalside location, but this time he was sketching the buildings and moored boats on the opposite side of the canal. The same young man approached him.

"Mr Agnew wants us to make arrangements," he said.

"Is there money involved?" asked Pinot without turning his head.

"I would like to buy that sketch."

"It's hardly a sketch. No more than a daub."

"So I'll give you forty euros for it."

"Make it forty-five and it's yours," answered Pinot.

The young man had the money ready and passed it over.

"I'll trust you," said Pinot as he pocketed the notes. "But I will check it later in case you've given me too much."

The young man hurried off without taking his purchase.

Pinot shook his head rather wistfully as he watched him go. "The young ones aren't trained as they used to be," he said, almost to himself. Then he added, "Or perhaps he's a real connoisseur," and his smile broadened.

Back in his apartment at lunchtime Pinot carefully separated the notes he'd been given. Between the two twenty-euro notes was a business card.

UK–N. Italy Industry Links
R. PARSONS, Regional Manager
Campo S. Giovanni Decollato
San Polo, Venice
APPOINTMENTS ONLY

Although Pinot had a good working knowledge of the city, he had to use his city map to locate the small Campo S. Giovanni Decallato. He assumed the Regional Manager wouldn't be available until three in the afternoon, so he took his time travelling across to the San Polo *sestiere*. However, he was wrong in his assumption about Mr Parsons, as he had obviously been looking out for him and accosted him just before he reached the office entrance.

"Mr Cordon? I think you are seeking some information from me."

"If you are Mr Parsons, then yes," answered Pinot.

They shook hands. "I would rather we talked in the open air," said Parsons, leading the way to an outside table at a café across the square. "I try not to mix business with other matters," he added.

"Probably wise," answered Pinot.

"Yes, only Charles Alsobri of the office staff knows about this."

"The young man who gave me your card this morning?"

"Yes, he was sent out from London almost a year ago. I was a little put out at the time – I prefer to recruit locally. However, I think he must have someone pushing him. Not that I've anything against him," he added hurriedly "He's a willing, personable lad."

"And he is to be my contact?"

"Yes, the short conversation you had two days ago confirmed that."

"So if we can sort out the all-important details of our contact method you'll be able to get back to your day job," said Pinot.

A waitress arrived at that moment and Parsons ordered two mineral waters before he turned again to Pinot.

"Where you were drawing this morning there are two cafés about thirty metres either side of where you were sitting, and one almost exactly opposite across the canal."

"Yes, I noticed them."

"Charles will walk past them every morning between eight-thirty and nine."

He waited while the waitress placed the drinks on the table. He then took four large playing cards showing the queens of the four suits and placed them beside the drinks before he continued. "You don't have to be there every day unless you have something to be reported to London. In that case, place them in a line with the queen of clubs furthest from you. Charles would then know that you would leave the message at the back of a folder of small paintings at your selling pitch one hour later."

"A pitch I haven't yet organised," broke in Pinot.

"That will be arranged. Charles will sort it out and he'll meet you where you were drawing today at this time next week."

"And the other cards?" asked Pinot.

"The red suits are meaningless, so you can use them or not. That's up to you. The queen of spades I don't suppose you'll ever use."

"But let's just suppose," said Pinot.

Parsons gathered up the cards and passed them across with the queen of spades on the top. Pinot placed them in his jacket pocket.

"If for some reason you needed to be out urgently, you'd place that card furthest from you and Agnew would do his damnedest."

"So if there's nothing to report I don't even have to be at one of those bars. In which case, how soon will Charles get sick of checking?"

"As I've said, he's willing and personable and, I've been informed, reliable. But I don't think you need worry on that score, Mr Cordon. I've been in this game long enough; I'll be checking on him. And by the way, make sure you use those bars randomly, no pattern."

"I too have been in this game, as you call it, a long time,' replied Pinot.

Parsons finished his drink and pushed himself to his feet. "Point taken. I'll be getting back to the mundane now. Good luck, Mr Cordon. Enjoy Venice."

"Just one more thing before you go," said Pinot. "I presume Charles will have holiday time occasionally, or be ill; what then?"

"You have no need to be worried about that. I personally will ensure that the arrangement is adhered to."

"Pompous Parsons," Pinot muttered to himself as he watched him walk across the square towards his office.

CHAPTER 5

Venice, June 18th 2012

Charles Alsobri worked as an administrator in the overstaffed, but rarely overworked, office of the grandly titled UK–Northern Italy Industry Links. His role of Industrial Relations Facilitator allowed him ample time to do Agnew's bidding. This involved him in sending regular appraisals of North Italian matters which might fit into a wider pattern of UK security. There was never any feedback except for the very welcome monthly payment into a Swiss bank account. In general the work was sometimes interesting, most times boring, but there was one aspect of it which he enjoyed – he was, and had been for almost a year now, the potential outlet of an agent named Pinot. His manager, Mr Parsons, had made the detailed arrangements for Pinot to make contact if that was ever necessary. Every morning between eight-thirty and nine Charles had to check out three canalside Venetian bars to see if Pinot was at one of them. More often than not, Pinot was not to be seen, in which case Charles could simply return to his administrative desk in Mr Parsons' little empire. At other times, in no particular pattern, he had been at one of the designated bars but there were no cards on his table, or if there were they were not in a meaningful pattern.

However, in the first three months there had been two occasions when the queen of clubs card was positioned, and Charles had had to act by checking out the pitch where Pinot displayed his art. On those occasions Charles felt a greater involvement, because he had informed Pinot that the corner near the Goppion bar would be a suitable place for him. Charles would find, among a selection of small prints, a coded message in an envelope which had to be sent to Agnew via Parsons. What it all meant he had no idea; indeed he had the feeling that it would be in his best interests not to know.

A further factor that he felt linked him to this world of Pinot's was that he arranged for him to use a disused warehouse to store his canvases. The place was owned by Janice, the English café owner, and Charles negotiated a good rental price.

Several more months went by without Charles having to take any action. Then Pinot began to appear less and less often at the bars, and Charles became less reliable in his checking routine. Unfortunately for Pinot, the one occasion when he had felt the need to use the other instruction involving the queen of spades card, Charles' attention was otherwise engaged. Pinot had vital information to pass to Agnew, but that knowledge placed him in grave danger; he needed help not only to get the message out but to get himself out. The arrangement failed. Charles had let him down.

* * *

On the morning of 27th of May 2015, Charles Alsobri met a young Italian woman and within two weeks they were seeing each other most evenings. Charles had little experience of women and he fell madly in love. As their relationship strengthened he did what a short time ago he would have considered unthinkable; he missed a couple of his regular Monday morning checks of the bars to spend a little more time with her.

At first he was worried that something big would happen and bring his world crashing down. He had no concerns for Pinot, as he'd never really known the man. But he found that almost every waking hour he was thinking of Carla, the girl he was prepared to die for. On the 18th of June, that was exactly what he did.

Her parents had a summer house in the Dolomites near the city of Trento which they rarely used. Twice Alsobri had ridden up there on his pride and joy, a 750 Ducati, and spent a passionate four days there with Carla. Early on this particular Wednesday morning, while she stayed for a few more days, he set off to head back to Venice. Although it was a wrench to leave Carla's charms, he was looking forward to the ride.

'Yes, I will take care," he promised her. He certainly did

for the two and a half kilometres down to the main road, but once he had joined it he opened up the throttle. The bike was a joy to handle at high speeds and the twisting downhill sections were just what he wanted.

He eased back a little as he approached the small town of Borgo, where he had been warned of the possible presence of the traffic police. There was no sign of them and as he left the outskirts of the town he became even more emboldened. Then, just as he was approaching a sweeping right-hand bend near the small settlement of Grigno, a timber lorry pulled out from a side road, completely blocking his path. A small truck was coming up the other carriageway; there was no escape route that way. Alsobri hit the brakes, and the bike slewed; the timber lorry continued its path and bike and rider crashed into it and were entangled with it for a hundred metres before the mangled remains of the bike and Alsobri's body were left creamed on the roadside. Neither the timber lorry nor the truck stopped.

When the traffic police, who had been enjoying a coffee in Borgo, arrived they were amazed to find that the rider was still alive, although it was obvious he was not going to survive his injuries. In the ambulance the paramedics did what they could, but he died before they reached the hospital at Trento. The police report stated: 'The road surface was good and dry, visibility was excellent. The skid marks suggest the motorcyclist was travelling at a speed well above the legal limit. There were no witnesses to the incident. Cause of the crash attributed to excess speed and rider error.'

At exactly nine o'clock on the morning that Alsobri died, Pinot was drinking coffee at a canalside bar. He had spread out his playing cards on the table in front of him with the queen of spades furthest from his body. He was waiting anxiously for his contact to appear. At nine-thirty he gathered together his cards, placed them in his bag, then walked rapidly in the direction of the Rialto.

CHAPTER 6

June 21st 2012, North Tyneside, England.

There were only two people who knew the number of Steve Cromarty's official mobile phone – Agnew and Macbride. When it rang at eight-thirty on the morning of the twenty-first of June, the voice was unmistakably that of Macbride. The message was brief, and to Steve it was both puzzling and deeply disturbing: "Dempsey has surfaced".

He knew the next call would be in exactly fifteen minutes. Time for him to try and consider just what those three words could mean. He was only aware of one Dempsey in Agnew's team of operatives, and, just over a year before, that man had been taken out by a hostile rocket attack in Jugoslavia. He'd even been to his funeral back in England. Now there were these three words about him surfacing. He decided it was pointless trying to make sense of it; he would wait for the second call.

He followed procedure and let it ring five times. It was Macbride again. "West door. Five minutes. J reg Merc. Bring the bag."

For Steve, it meant another moving out time. The flat would be sanitised and made ready for immediate use for the next occupant, which might or might not be Steve. A note explaining his absence from the library was probably already waiting for Katherine. None of it would have been done by Agnew, but all of it would have been organised by him.

Steve had used the west door the previous day, but it didn't matter as he used the three exits randomly. He presumed that Macbride was aware that the west door was the one nearest to the main road. The Merc was waiting there. As he approached it the boot lid slowly opened and he carefully stowed his bag before sliding into the rear passenger seat beside Macbride.

Macbride leant forward and moved the glass panel so he could speak to the driver. "The airport," he said. The driver gave the faintest of nods and smoothly pulled the car away. Macbride closed the panel then, turning to Steve, he said, "No more than forty-five minutes from here but plenty of time for me to fill you in with some details about a man called Pinot." There was just the glimmer of a smile before he added, "Before that he was known as Dempsey. The Dempsey you knew."

Steve settled himself in his seat while the driver executed an excellent U-turn, despite heavy oncoming traffic from Whitley Bay, and headed the car out towards

Earsdon village. It was only when they were leaving the A186 for the A19N that he asked the question which had been gnawing at him since he'd received Macbride's first call.

"So what's this about Dempsey?"

Macbride shifted his body so he was turned towards Steve. He spoke slowly, obviously choosing his words with care.

"I've been told that the last time you saw him he was setting off to disappear, although you didn't know that."

Steve was listening intently.

"Taking gold to Kosovan rebels was never to be the final outcome of that journey," continued Macbride, "at least not for Dempsey. As well as the gold a dead body, with Dempsey's name tag round its neck, had been loaded into the back of the truck. It was all planned that Dempsey should leave the vehicle and then be picked up by another before the rocket attack took place."

"A model of timing and execution," said Steve.

"Couldn't be faulted," agreed Macbride, "although I might disagree with some of your wording. But the main point is that when the first vehicle was hit and virtually obliterated Dempsey was already on his way to a changed identity and a changed role. He became Pinot Cordon and went into deep cover in Venice, making a living of sorts as an artist selling his work to tourists."

Steve, with an image of the coffin at Mounsett crematorium clear in his memory, had to make a rapid mental readjustment. "So why has he been brought out so quickly, and what's it got to do with me?" he asked.

"That's the whole point of this assignment, Steve. We

didn't bring him up. As you know anyone put into deep cover remains there until they're brought out. Of course, that might never happen; could be a lifetime. They always know where there's a contact, but to use it to get out you'd need the father and mother of a reason. And at the moment we can't think of one."

"I take it Dempsey, or Pinot, has made his own decision."

"That's exactly what he's done and we don't know why," answered Macbride. "But because he made the move we need to know. Agnew has shifted this to top priority."

"And just where do I fit into this?"

"You fly out from Newcastle to Venice by way of Schiphol at eleven o'clock our time. It's all booked for you and there's an apartment for you in the Cannareggio district near where Pinot was living." He pulled an envelope out of his inside pocket and handed it across. "Don't bother checking. All you need is there."

Steve nodded. "So I make contact, then what?"

"If it was only that simple. First of all you have to find him."

Steve's expression was a mixture of incredulity and disbelief. "What you mean is, he's surfaced and you've lost him."

"That's one way of looking at it," growled Macbride, "but it's not Agnew's. He reckons that whatever caused him to surface was too dangerous for him to hang around waiting for us to reach him. But we need to know."

Steve leaned back into the soft leather seat. Glancing out of the window, he saw they were passing the White Swan at Dinnington. They were making good time. He and Katherine had enjoyed a number of pleasant evenings there which had had very little to do with his Hanseatic League study.

He turned again to Macbride. "Dempsey must have had..."

"Let's stick with the name Pinot," broke in Macbride.

"OK, what does Pinot's contact have to tell us?"

"Unfortunately he's not in a position to tell us anything," said Macbride. "He was involved in a road accident five days ago in the Trentino area of Northern Italy. Apparently a timber lorry smeared him and his bike all over the road. No witnesses, so it might or might not have been an accident. He didn't survive the journey to hospital."

"Bit of bad luck for him and for us," said Steve. "What about his address, or is that too simple?"

"He hasn't been seen there for almost a week now," answered Macbride.

"But there must have been some sort of back-up."

"Yeah. The bloke who runs the legitimate cover business in Venice is Robert Vincent Parsons. But apparently he rarely stirs himself from the office, so about a year ago a young chap was sent out to do the legwork for him. He was the one killed on the bike. The only help Parsons could give us was the name of an English woman who rented Pinot a place to store his art work. She's married to an Italian and they own a café/bar at the junction of the Rio Terra Leonardo and the Rio Terra Farsetti."

Steve made a stab at the spelling as he made a note of the location.

"Well it's a start. Does she have a name?"

"Janice Asconi."

"Not a lot to go on," said Steve.

"That's why my travelling bag is also in the boot," answered Macbride.

"I did notice it. Does that mean we're going out together?"

Macbride gave him one of his withering looks. "You should know by now just how particular I am about my travelling companions."

"Just like me," answered Steve.

The comment was ignored. "We'll be at the airport in five minutes. You'll be dropped off there. Then," and he nodded at the driver's back, "he's taking me down to Manchester, where I'll meet up with Agnew and we'll fly out direct to Vicenza and then the Americans will take us by car to Trieste."

Steve raised his eyebrows and allowed only a hint of sarcasm in his voice.

"So this is big league stuff, if Agnew is getting personally involved."

"He's done more than his share in the past," answered Macbride sharply. "At his age he prefers to pull the strings at a distance, but it seems there may have been some sort of American connection in Pinot's surfacing, and only Agnew can tackle that."

"And if he gets some information you'll pass it on to me, then the two of you will high-tail it back to England."

"Only half right, Steve. I'll be staying on. I know where you'll be staying and I expect to catch up with you there, probably late afternoon two days from now."

Minutes later Steve was dropped off at the entrance to the terminal building of Newcastle International Airport. He had not expected any last-minute instructions, and he was right. He pulled his bag out of the car's boot just moments before it swept away.

CHAPTER 7

Over the years Steve had developed an almost pathological hatred of large commercial airports. Despite the blandishments of expensive retail stores and the alluring adverts temptingly suggesting that a visit to a far-flung place should be next on your itinerary, for him it simply reinforced the fact that you weren't there now. Instead you were one of thousands sitting almost comatose and wishing you were anywhere else. Quick – perhaps; carefree – never; boring – almost to the point of being brain dead.

Newcastle International, despite its name, was still small enough to be bearable, at least for an hour or two, but unfortunately Amsterdam's Schiphol was something else, a world hub, processing tens of thousands of people who all ended up staring at indicator boards like lost souls. Steve needed to have some level of control of his own life. He looked forward to being in Venice, even though initially he would be working inside the parameters determined by Agnew. A wry smile had crossed his face when he had checked through his itinerary; as he'd expected, there was a ticket for the slowest route into the city. There was to be no James Bond-type water taxi racing across the lagoon, bouncing over the washes of other speeding craft. Agnew was a brilliant man, well organised and thorough, but his Yorkshire roots meant he kept a tight rein on his department's expenditure. As a result it was a forty-five minute crossing on an Alilaguna water bus that Steve had to take from the Marco Polo airport harbour. The brief notes he'd been given with his itinerary warned him that there were four lines that crossed the lagoon to the city, and of the four only the Arancia line would take him to the Guglie stop on the Cannareggio canal.

He was fortunate in that within a few minutes of completing the short walk to the harbour it was the orange line boat which arrived. It quickly filled up with tourists, mainly young, presumably operating on a tight budget, and some elderly who perhaps preferred the more leisurely form of transport. Steve was there simply following Agnew's instructions, but on reflection he thought a low-key approach was probably best – this way his entry to the city was not likely to draw any unwelcome attention.

At the Guglie stop he was among about a dozen people who left the boat. He took his time while the others went their separate ways, then he walked away to the Tre Archi bridge, crossed it, and walked back along the *fondamenta* to the Tre Archi ristorante. From there it was easy to find his apartment, which was on the second floor in an apartment block bordering a narrow side canal. By the time he'd checked it out, which didn't take long, and stowed his few possessions, he reckoned an evening meal in the restaurant around the corner would be a reasonable move; the search for Pinot could begin in earnest tomorrow.

Andrea, the young restaurant owner, was both enthusiastic and welcoming, and he spoke excellent English. He explained to Steve that the bulk of his customers didn't arrive until after nine o'clock so he was quite happy to chat. If only Steve had had a better knowledge of English Premier League football, Andrea would have been in his element. As it was the conversation was limited, although Steve did mention that an old friend of his, name of Pinot Cordon, had moved to Venice just over a year ago.

"I promised I'd look him up if ever I got here, but I've lost his address," he explained. "The name Cannareggio rings a bell and I think he said it was near the Ghetto area, but that's all I can remember."

Andrea, in dramatic Italian fashion, flung his arms wide and seemed to be genuinely distraught that he was unable to help.

"I live out in Mestre, over the causeway," he explained, "so I don't have a great knowledge of people who live in Cannareggio unless they are regular customers of mine, and I don't know anyone called Pinot."

Steve was neither surprised nor despondent; he could hardly expect Pinot to be handed to him on a plate. He turned the conversation to the question of food.

"This is going to be my first meal in Venice," he said.

Andrea nodded and waited.

"I've been travelling most of the day, so I only want a main course with a decent wine and a reasonable price. What would you recommend? And remember I'm renting just round the corner." He gave a smile to indicate it wasn't really a threat.

Andrea nodded again to show he fully understood the situation. He seemed to consider for a moment, then said, "The *fritto misto* is *buonissimo*, and a bottle of Müller Thurgau. I am sure you will not be disappointed."

Steve leaned back in his chair. "Bring it on, Andrea."

Andrea smiled. "And I'll ask around among my regulars if any of them know your friend."

"Good man," said Steve.

Over the next hour the restaurant gradually filled, and Steve was very aware of the general friendly atmosphere and the mutual regard Andrea and his staff had with the customers. However, when Andrea arrived with Steve's meal he shook his head. "I'm sorry, no-one seems to know your friend, but Cannareggio is the biggest of the sestieri and many people live here. Even around the Ghetto area."

"Don't worry," said Steve. "I'm here for a week or so. I'll do some asking around and might be lucky."

The food and wine did not disappoint. "You'll be seeing me again," Steve told Andrea after he had accepted a glass of Nardini grappa on the house. He then made the short journey back to his apartment. He had made no progress regarding Pinot, but it was very early days. The real search would begin tomorrow.

CHAPTER 8

The next morning did not bring the cloudless blue sky Steve had expected. Instead low cloud trailed along the surface of the canal and the working barges seemed to appear almost wraith-like as they slowly made their way along to deliver to the bars and restaurants. Despite the general damp atmosphere, Steve spent some time under the shelter of an awning watching their progress. As well as the barges there were other essential watercraft; police, fire, and ambulance launches, some of them with blue flashing lights and high-pitched sirens indicating emergency calls requiring the need for a clear passage. There was also an early morning *vaporetto* edging its way into the Crea stop. The whole scene brought it home to him that he was in a unique city where life depended on the canals and the boats.

If the weather had been warm, bright and sunny he

would probably have had a more positive outlook about the task he had been given, but the grey, dull morning caused any enthusiasm he might have had to slowly seep away.

Where to start the search? Macbride had given him two names and the work address of one of them; Janice Asconi. So the choice was made for him. A careful scrutiny of the city street plan in the apartment had shown him that this would be the easy part. At the Guglie bridge he could turn left and follow the Strada Nova and two hundred yards down there he'd come across Janice's bar. This meant he would also be following part of the route taken by hundreds of tourists making their way to two of the major sights of the city; the Rialto bridge and, further on, St Mark's square and basilica. As a result, even at a very damp, chilly nine o'clock in the morning, he found himself caught up in a seething mass of mainly young people, some of them weighed down with rucksacks big enough to transport an entire wardrobe. These he could wend his way around, but there were some places where he found his way blocked by others determinedly taking 'selfie' photographs of themselves and their friends using the extending poles which the ever-enterprising street corner entrepreneurs were selling.

Curbing his impatience, as after all he had no other plan than to have an espresso doppio and a brioche for his breakfast, he reached the Goppion bar by nine-thirty. The young waiter who served him informed him that the English lady was busy on the phone dealing with suppliers.

"There's no hurry," said Steve. "Just ask her if I could have a word when she's free."

The sun was just beginning to break through the cloud,

and Steve was pleased he had chosen a seat well inside the shading canopy. As he ate his brioche he amused himself trying to guess the nationalities of the passers-by. He could well understand that if you were looking to disappear even for just a short time, you should choose a city; if it was for a long time, you should choose a city with a population that changes almost daily, one where a different race or colour or language would not cause any comment. Agnew had chosen Pinot's deep cover very well.

"Hello. I'm Janice. You asked to see me." She had a pleasant, open smile. Steve liked her.

"Pleased to meet you. I'm Steve. Steve Cromarty." He pushed himself to his feet and Janice smiled as he proffered a handshake.

"It's a while since I've had such a formal introduction," she said.

"That's because I want to be formal." Then he added, to avoid being considered too business-like, "You haven't lost your accent."

"At heart I'm still the girl from Wiltshire. But what brought you here? Do we have a mutual friend?"

"I hope so," answered Steve. He hurried on as he saw her puzzled expression. "A man called Pinot."

"Well I do know a man of that name. Not terribly well, and he might not be the man you're looking for. If it is him, he rents an old warehouse from me just around the corner about fifty yards from here. He stores his art stuff there."

"I wondered if he'd kept up his art," lied Steve.

"Yes, he's pretty good, at least for the tourist market. Not that I'm an expert but I don't think he sells many, although he must make enough to make it worth his while."

Just for a moment Steve remembered the consignment of gold coins that had been loaded into the vehicle that Dempsey had boarded with the Kosovans. Perhaps selling his art to tourists was never a priority.

"I would have thought he would be as serious about it as he is with most things," answered Steve.

"You probably know him better than I do," she replied. "But sometimes he just leaves the easels out all day and goes off with his friends. Then he'll come back, push them into his store and go off, presumably to his place."

"He always was a trusting soul. But I've lost touch with where he lives now. I know it's Cannareggio, but it's a big area."

"Can't help you there. I've never known his address, but it's possible that one of the group he wanders off and puts the world to rights with might know."

Steve smiled. "He obviously hasn't changed. He always liked nothing better than a good argument. A discussion, he always called it."

"Yes, I think we know the same Pinot," said Janice. "I must go now and do some work, or the staff will think I'm leaving it all to them. It looks as though Pinot's not making an appearance today, but you might catch up with him and his pals at the Rialto market, probably in the Do Mori bar. There's usually six of them as well as Pinot. If he's not there, look for a very tall man with a trimmed beard. He's Sergio, the ringleader I call him. Retired from the Air Force, I think. Must go now. See you again I hope."

"Sure," said Steve. He threw back the rest of his coffee, pushed a ten-euro note into the hand of the waiter and joined the crowd moving down the street. Already he was pleased with the morning's work. Janice had been ready to talk and he felt sure he could return and have a further chat; and now he had another name: Sergio.

Twenty minutes easy walking brought him to the Ca D'Oro vaporetto stop and, pushing his way onto a packed waterbus, he travelled down to the Rialto. If he thought he had been in a crowded thoroughfare in the Strada Nova it was nothing compared to the crush of bodies on the bridge and then on the Ruga degli Speziali which led to the vegetable and fish markets.

He made two failed attempts to ask for directions to the Do Mori bar before a large, buxom American woman overheard him. "I'll take you darling," she said with a smile, and she was as good as her word. At the entrance he thanked her and gently removed his arm from her grasp. "I'm here most days," she said as she weaved her way along the narrow street.

The bar was located just off the fish market. Its reputation as one of the haunts of Casanova would have made it a tourist 'must', but probably because of its lack of seating, other than a few upturned wine barrels, most of its clientele were regulars and Venetian.

As the bar straddled the width of the block of buildings there were two entrances, one in each calle. Steve checked out one door, but there was no group of six or seven men and certainly not the tall man Janice had mentioned. He made his way round the block, past the doorway of a pet shop, which was guarded by a suspicious terrier of indeterminate breed, and a small modern art gallery.

Just as he turned the corner, fortune smiled on him. Several men, mostly elderly and obviously a group of friends, were turning into the bar, and one of them fitted Janice's description of the retired Air Force man. Steve hurried after them, concerned that they might just be strolling in through one door and out through the other. However, when he made his way in they had all formed into a group beside the broad counter and small glasses were being pushed across to them already filled with *vino rosso.* The group were obviously well known to the barman.

Steve ordered a glass of the same wine, on the assumption that the regulars would be drinking something reasonable. The group of six were congregated around one half of the bar counter area, so the barman placed Steve's drink further along the counter beyond two glass cabinets in which various fish sandwiches were displayed. As a result, although he was unable to move into the orbit of the group, he could see them more clearly. Pinot was not among them.

While he was considering his options, the group suddenly downed their drinks and left the bar calling 'Ciao, Rosario' over their shoulders.

"Was that Sergio, the tall, bearded man?" Steve asked the barman.

"Yes, that's Sergio," answered the barman as he gathered up the used glasses.

"I thought he'd moved away to Umbria when he retired," said Steve, anxious to extend the conversation.

"Not Sergio. We need security surveillance men even more these days so I think he's still involved in some way."

"Oh, I always thought he was Air Force."

"That must have been a long time ago. It's satellite tracking these days, but don't ask me what that is."

"I don't know either, too high tech for me."

He had another glass of vino and then, when a number of workers from the market came in and the barman was busy with them, he waved farewell and walked out into the street. There was no sign of Sergio and his group, but Steve was happy enough with the morning's work. Rather than push his luck too hard he decided to wait until the morning, when he could have another coffee and possibly a further profitable chat with Janice.

In the meantime he braved the crowded vaporetto once more and travelled up to the Ferrovia stop. He'd decided to check out the railway station to get a better feel for the place and its links with other cities. But before that he had a light lunch in a nearby restaurant; it was reasonable food, but not as good as Andrea's and at a price which would have caused Agnew to wince.

CHAPTER 9

The Santa Lucia railway station was very busy. Smartly-dressed businessmen and women, most of them carrying equally smart leather briefcases, were striding purposefully to or from the trains while groups of tourists, having to wend their way around the large queues patiently waiting their turn at the overworked information desks, were making a hesitant, halting progression towards the exits.

After spending half an hour wandering around the station concourse noting the entry gates for the various platforms and then checking the boards of arrivals and departures, Steve felt he had added to his knowledge of Venice and its rail links. It confirmed his view that the city still had a strategic position linking the major European centres with the Balkan states and beyond. Perhaps the centuries-old migration routes, disrupted by the First and

Second World Wars, were once more assuming their historic role, but this time for far larger numbers and with the possibility of terrorists being among them. Was this what had caused Pinot to surface?

Steve decided to make his way back to his apartment, but on the way he resolved to look out for one or two bars where he could have a cold beer and hope that the name Pinot might mean something to the staff. It was a slim chance, but if he was to be found it was worth a shot.

By now the cool, damp morning was but a distant memory and everyone was suffering in the heat, including the young men manning stalls selling T-shirts and football shirts named and numbered for all the stars in the major European leagues. Steve hurried down the station steps, ignored the several vaporetto boarding areas and, keeping in the shade of the buildings as far as possible, he turned left and followed the crowd down the main thoroughfare, the Rio Terra Lista di Spagna. There were one or two bars which were tempting, but he didn't think Pinot would have frequented this part of the Cannareggio area – too crowded, too touristy – so he continued to the Ponte delle Guglie. There he turned left along the Fondamenta Venier and then the Fondamenta Savorgnan. At this point the canal-side pavement became broader, allowing more room for the cafés to spread tables and chairs. The general atmosphere was more relaxed and easy-going, helped by a refreshing breeze blowing down from the lagoon.

Now out of the main throng of tourists, he found himself amongst groups of students obviously making their way to or from lectures. This part of the city housed three major departments of the Università di Ca Foscari. Glancing into the window of the student bookshop and taking note of some of the logos on the T-shirts being worn, he judged Economics, Business Management and Environmental Sciences to be the areas of study. Although Pinot's student days were long past and his interests in languages and linguistics did not appear to be catered for here, Steve felt he would have been more at home in this sort of atmosphere. He also just had a hunch that Environmental Sciences might have some involvement that might lead to something interesting. Anyway he reckoned he had nothing to lose, and a couple of cold beers to gain, from trying his luck at the bars.

The first bar, which was clearly very popular with young students of both sexes, provided the beer but no useful information, although the waiters seemed anxious to help. However, Steve did not see that after he had spoken to the staff a small group of older men also quizzed them, and within a few minutes two of these men left the bar.

The next bar was equally unproductive in terms of information, but the young woman at the next bar, the Parlamento, remembered an older man called Pinot who had come there a few times over the past few months. He had drunk only glasses of mineral water and sat on his own at one of the outside tables furthest from the bar entrance. He always seemed to be playing some sort of card game with a small number of unusually large playing cards, which he took out of his shoulder bag and spread on the table. It was the playing cards that she remembered him by. When pressed, she did say that she got the impression he was waiting for someone to join him, but as far as she knew no one ever did.

"I knew him a long time ago and as I'm here for a few days I thought I'd try to get in touch, but he's moved on from the address I had for him," Steve explained.

"Sorry, I can't help you there, but I'll have a word with Gianni. He talks to most people, so he might know." She disappeared into the dark interior of the bar, but before Steve could build up his hopes she reappeared, shaking her head. "He doesn't know where he lives," she said, "but when I mentioned the cards, that jogged his memory. He said the only other time he'd seen him it was outside the Anticha Adelaide bar."

Steve pulled out his city plan and she ringed the area where he would find the bar.

"Gianni also said Pinot wasn't playing cards there but was sharing a table with a tall, bearded man who looked as though he'd been in the armed services. I don't know why he thought that, but that's what he said."

"And that man never came here?"

"Not that I know of, but..." She shrugged.

"Perhaps if I talked to Gianni," suggested Steve.

"I'm sorry," she replied. "We encourage people to sit and drink coffee or wine and chat amongst themselves. For hours if they want." She waved an arm in the general direction of a small group of elderly women who were sitting at an outside table. "But I have a job to do, so I must get on."

"You've already been most helpful," said Steve. He gave her a pleasant smile and pushed a ten euro note into her hand.

His intention had been to return to his apartment, but he was now intrigued by the fact that both Pinot and the bearded man, who had to be Sergio, the man he had seen in

Do Mori, had met at other places without the rest of the group. He decided to visit the Adelaide bar, which was now marked on his city plan, even though it meant retracing his steps and rejoining the tourist trail. He felt sure there would be a quicker route known only to the locals. He was already aware from his short time in the city that to get from A to B involved crossing so many bridges and following the twists and turns of so many small canals that becoming lost was the most likely outcome.

He was almost back to the Guglie bridge when a swarthy, heavily-tattooed, middle-aged man overtook him and then turned and grasped his arm. Steve halted, looked directly at the man and smiled as he in turn gripped the other's wrist and then slightly tightened and twisted his grip.

"I think not, my friend," he said, keeping eye contact.

"Sorry sir," the man said, releasing Steve's arm. "I'm Gianni Rossi from the Parlamento. Gloria works for me. I couldn't talk back there but I think you should know your friend Pinot seems to be involved with some, er, I'm not sure how you would say, *persone indesiderabili.* Not good men. You understand? And I also think he is frightened of them." Gianni quickly glanced around, obviously anxious not to be seen talking to Steve. "I must get back," he added and then hurried back towards his bar.

Steve made his way up to the bridge, halted at the top and leaned on its smooth, stone parapet, looking along the canal towards the next bridge. It was the one near his apartment, the Tre Archi. He could see Gianni was almost back at his bar. He would have liked to ask him more about the 'undesirables' he'd mentioned, but he would find another opportunity. In the meantime some sort of picture was beginning to emerge about Pinot, although the major task of locating him still remained, and until that happened his reason for surfacing was unknown.

He was just turning to make his way off the bridge when he caught sight of two men coming out of an alleyway near the Parlamento. They confronted Gianni, who made an attempt to sidestep them, but one of them grabbed him and there seemed to be some sort of brief argument before the second man stepped in and Gianni crumpled to the pavement. At the distance he was from them, about a hundred metres, Steve couldn't be sure, but he thought he saw the flash of a knife blade. The men then turned and headed back into the alleyway and were lost to sight.

Gianni had pushed himself up onto his knees. Gloria and one of the customers ran across to him and together they helped him to his feet and supported him as he staggered into the bar. Steve moved off the bridge and strolled along to the MQ 10 bar, which was almost directly opposite to the Parlamento. There he ordered a beer and waited and watched.

He ran over in his mind the stabbing episode; he felt sure there had been a knife. The almost casual way in which the two men had left the scene suggested to him that they were practised, and when after half an hour no ambulance launch had appeared along the canal, he felt sure the stabbing had simply been a warning to Gianni. It was unlikely that he would get any further information from that source. That was something of a blow to Steve's plans.

More worrying was that somehow the 'undesirables' were clearly aware that he was asking questions about the whereabouts of Pinot. He cast his mind back to the people he had talked to, Andrea, Janice and the Do Mori barman, but all three had seemed to want to help him. Of course he had to admit that they too had made enquiries on his behalf and it was possible word had reached the ears of these undesirables.

He decided to return to his apartment and wait for Macbride. Although it was still stifling hot, he decided to retrace his steps to the vaporetto stops outside the Ferrovia. He thought there was just an outside chance he might come across the two attackers. However, amongst the crush of people, he soon changed his mind and went for a vaporetto.

The first boat to arrive which went along the Cannareggio canal was the No. 52, and as it then went on to the islands of Murano and Burano, it was almost packed, mainly with tourists. Steve stepped aboard and stood on the open deck area. Even there, with the throng of heavily-perspiring fellow passengers all around, he was glad he only had to bear it for the two stops to the Tre Archi bridge.

CHAPTER 10

The same day as Steve travelled to Venice via Amsterdam, Agnew and Macbride flew direct from Manchester to Treviso. They rarely travelled together, but as on the few other occasions, they followed Agnew's rules. Macbride went through the check-in and security sections several minutes ahead of Agnew and, although both had seats in the economy class section, they were in well-separated rows. On arrival in Treviso they were picked up by separate cars which took slightly different routes to reach the A4 motorway for the drive to their final destination, the Castello di Miramare, about eight kilometres north west of Trieste.

It was mid evening when they arrived, within minutes of each other, to be greeted by Admiral Brosnich, the Commander of the American surveillance team, who occupied an annexe located well away from the grounds, which had been open to the public for the past ten years.

"Good to meet up with you again, Agnew." Brosnich was a heavily-built man with iron-grey hair closely cropped to a bullet-like head. Forty years ago he had probably been a formidable quarterback, thought Macbride. He was wearing US Army uniform with four rows of medal ribbons. Agnew by contrast was wearing a dark grey suit and a blue tie with a fine white diagonal stripe. He had no need to show the trappings of power - he had a natural air of authority.

Macbride noticed that there was no attempt at a handshake and although the greeting was polite enough, it was decidedly cool.

"Surprised you're still here," responded Agnew.

"I presume by that you mean TRUST, not me personally," countered Brosnich.

Agnew gave a non-committal nod and then turned to Macbride. "This man is the reason why we are here. He, more than anyone else, has his finger on the flickering, erratic pulse of the whole Adriatic region," he said. He turned back to Brosnich and smiled. Macbride saw the American visibly preen at the compliment; Agnew was a past master at handling delicate situations and smoothing ruffled feathers.

"I've cleared my diary for the first half of tomorrow morning so we can have our discussion then," said Brosnich. "Does that fit with your schedule?"

"That sounds just fine", answered Agnew, just as another uniformed man entered the room.

"Good. Then Lieutenant Northcott here will show you to your rooms."

"Would there be any food to be had this late?" asked Macbride.

"I'm sure he has already seen to that," answered Brosnich rather curtly.

The two rooms Northcott showed them to were on the first floor, linked by a small lounge area with armchairs and a coffee table where an excellent small buffet was laid out. The two men made rapid inroads into the cold meats and sandwiches, while Macbride drank a half bottle of Pinot Grigio and Agnew chose a glass of San Benedetto. That explained Brosnich's response to my question, thought Macbride.

All three rooms had picture windows giving excellent views north to the small village of Grignano. Agnew stood looking out across the bay while Macbride finished his wine. Then he turned with a quizzical smile on his face.

"I think I saw the slightest of glazes come across your eyes when Brosnich mentioned trust downstairs. Is that correct?" he asked.

Macbride nodded. "I know they've had a place here since the back end of the Second World War, but the word didn't mean anything to me."

"Well let me explain. It has nothing to do with confidence or belief in someone or something. It's written in capital letters, T R U S T, and it's the acronym for Trieste United States Troops. It was coined by the Americans when their forces had this place as their base from 1947 until they moved out in 1954."

"Except they're still here," added Macbride.

"That's true. Officially TRUST has been long gone, but unofficially a surveillance team has remained here and

Brosnich has headed it up for the past seven or eight years."

"So you know him from then?"

"Yes. He hadn't been in post long when he tried to pull rank on me and I wouldn't co-operate. You must have noticed his welcome when we arrived. He still hasn't forgotten."

"About Dempsey, I assume," said Macbride.

"That's right. He was aware of Dempsey's language skills and his almost encyclopaedic knowledge of the whole region and realised he would be a great asset on their team, so he wanted him and I refused. In fact it would be more correct to say the British Government refused. They had invested heavily in him and were not prepared to give him up. Unfortunately, now, several years down the line, Pinot, as he is now, has broken cover of his own accord."

Agnew stopped speaking for a moment, apparently entranced by the view of the coast. Then he turned, looked at Macbride, and grimaced before continuing. "And how were we informed of that?"

Macbride knew it was a rhetorical question. "Don't tell me," he replied.

"Yes," Agnew replied wearily. "Somehow one of Brosnich's people in Venice got wind of it and informed Brosnich and he gloatingly informed us. And we need to be able to contact that person."

"So that's why we're here," put in Macbride.

"Exactly, but it's doubly unfortunate that Brosnich is still in charge. So now, cap in hand, to get the information we need, I'll have to tread extremely carefully."

"He certainly didn't strike me as the forgive and forget type," said Macbride.

Agnew poured himself another half glass of water before he answered. "True, and he certainly doesn't deal in gratuitous information, but who does? However, I think I can persuade him. If not it'll have to go higher, but that would take more time, and time might be in short supply."

"Nothing I can do?" asked Macbride, although he knew it was really a statement, not a question.

"No. Have an early breakfast, walk round the grounds – they're well worth seeing – and I'll talk with Brosnich. If it all goes as planned I'll see you before I go back home and you'll meet up with Cromarty in Venice. If it doesn't, I'll have to rejig things and let you both know."

Next morning Macbride was up before seven and breakfasted, and by seven-thirty he was idly wandering around the grounds, knowing the general public weren't allowed in for at least another hour. He found it very pleasant to be able to enjoy the mix of formal gardens and wooded areas with stands of mature trees and shrubs which had been brought from the four corners of the globe with no expense spared. He studied a visitor information board and admired the view across the Gulf of Trieste towards the National Park area of the delta of the river Isonzo. The original owners, an Austrian Archduke and his Belgian princess bride, had certainly picked a good spot, mused Macbride, as well as having an almost bottomless pot of money to spend on the building.

He turned onto a path leading back to the building and wondered what progress Agnew was making in reaching some sort of agreement or accommodation with Brosnich. They desperately needed as much information as possible about who Pinot might have had contact with in Venice. Without that, the chance of he and Cromarty locating Pinot and learning the reason for his surfacing was almost nil. At the very least Agnew had to get a name.

Macbride was back in his room shortly before ten, packed and ready for Agnew to return and inform him of the outcome of his meeting. He did not have long to wait. Agnew was not one to show his feelings, so when he came into Macbride's room there was no outward sign of success or failure.

"You got a name from him?"

Agnew nodded. "Eventually I did. But only after we'd had a lengthy and detailed discussion about links between British, Italian and Croatian Mafia cells. I can't say I'm fully happy with the outcome and I won't know if I've paid too high a price in terms of information given until we know the reason for Pinot's surfacing."

"I'm sure it'll be something crucial," said Macbride.

"It will have to be even better than that," answered Agnew.

"And the name?"

"A woman called Claudia Mancini. I'll give you her details as we drive out to Treviso. I'll be flying back to London from there, as there are some important ends I have to tie up, so you and Cromarty will have to sort this and quickly. If you don't – well…" he spread his hands, palms up. "But you will. I have every confidence."

On the car journey to Treviso Agnew was at first silent, obviously lost in his own thoughts about what he had to see to back in London. Eventually Macbride asked about Claudia Mancini.

"It's not a lot, but it should be enough for you to go on. She's thirty-two, a widow. No children. Her husband, an American, was a United Nations casualty in Serbia. She's been an agent for the US for about five years. According to Brosnich she's good. She lives on the mainland with her disabled mother near a place called Marano. She travels to work in Venice four days a week, Tuesday to Friday, usually by car but sometimes by train as there's a main line railway station at Marano. Her regular contact with Brosnich takes place every second Friday, or more frequently if necessary. How, I don't know. That's Brosnich's affair."

"And what is her normal work in Venice?" asked Macbride.

"She's one of those extremely important people who act as temporary personal assistants for the rich and famous who are spending time in the city unbeknown to the press and paparazzi guys."

"Interesting."

"And one other thing," added Agnew. "I'm told she's a head turner, to put it mildly."

"So how, where and when do we meet up with her? That will be Cromarty's first question," said Macbride.

"Brosnich was vague on this. She'll probably be being briefed about the pair of you now, but it's got to appear casual, not official. Don't forget they don't want her role compromised in any way. But she seems to start her working days about ten o'clock with a coffee at a bar in the Campo della Pescaria, which is near the Rialto markets, as she knows the family who own the place. She always carries a small leather briefcase and she dresses to impress."

"And after her coffee?"

"She only acts for the top six hotels, so whichever one needs her."

They were now approaching Treviso and within minutes the car was pulling into the airport entrance. As Agnew got out of the car he turned and leant in towards Macbride. "You know the importance of this, so make sure Cromarty stays focused. I know what he can be like. But I also know what the pair of you can do."

Macbride nodded, but Agnew was already striding away.

The journey to Venice was a silent one. The driver had his instructions and Macbride had his own thoughts. He'd been in the city on several occasions, never as a tourist, so he had more than a good working knowledge of the routes and haunts used by the locals. More than that, he had some trusted Italian contacts, if they were still in place. The first he would be looking to trace was a man called Sergio. A smile flitted across Macbride's face as he brought to mind long grappa-fuelled evenings and remembered that Sergio, of all people, was the one who could cover or uncover tracks. An important man, and possibly a very useful one.

CHAPTER 11

The first thing Steve did when he entered the apartment was to go across to the small balcony overlooking the canal. He opened the full-length windows and felt a slight but very welcome movement of air. Below him the working barges were still plying their trade, and it struck Steve how different this canal was from the world-renowned Grand Canal. The Cannareggio had no fine palazzi bordering it, but its utilitarian 'busy-ness' gave it a special, unique atmosphere, and the pavements along both sides enabled you to walk its full length from the Guglie bridge to where it met the lagoon. It was a canal that seemed to belong to the local people. Steve liked both the canal and the area.

By leaning out onto the metal railing of the balcony he could just see, to his left, the lagoon, about two hundred yards beyond the Tre Archi bridge. But for the moment, that didn't particularly interest him. He was sure Macbride, when he did arrive, would approach from the other direction, so he carefully positioned a mirror, taken from the tiny bathroom, so that sitting in the easy chair, with a beer on a side table, he could both relax and be observant. He knew Macbride wouldn't expect anything less.

Macbride, for his part, approached as Steve had expected, but once he was in the communal entrance hall he waited a good five minutes before climbing the stairs to the second floor. He then took care to make a silent entry, although he felt sure Steve would be aware of him.

As he pushed the door open, he deftly caught the full beer can that Steve lobbed over to him. Both men smiled. Macbride opened his can, raised it towards Steve and then drank deeply.

"I don't suppose this is to celebrate you having found our Pinot."

"Correct, but I haven't been idle," said Steve.

Macbride ignored the remark and cast his eyes around the room. "How does this place suit you?" he asked.

"It's not five star, but it will do for now. But it's not made for two."

"Now when did you ever concern yourself about my welfare, Steve? My bag's already at a rooming place near Janice's bar. I've just called to give you the information Agnew managed to get out of Brosnich."

During the next half-hour they brought each other up to date with what they'd learned. Steve made a mental note of the description of Claudia but deliberately refrained from making any comment.

"A reasonable day's work," said Macbride, not grudgingly

but without any real enthusiasm. "Particularly as your Sergio fits the description of a man I met here two years ago and we had some good times together. In fact he's probably the one I'll be searching out tomorrow."

"Sounds like a lucky coincidence. But how did the two of you meet back then?" asked Steve.

"At the time I thought it was by chance, but afterwards I wondered if Agnew had had something to do with it. It was in a bar."

"Where else?" asked Steve, opening another two cans. Macbride took the hint.

"OK, we've got the time. I'll tell you about him. The bar was just off the Via Garibaldi in the Castello sestiere that's getting down towards the Arsenale."

"I've heard of it, but I don't know it," said Steve. "The station down as far as Janice's bar, and across to the Do Mori. That's as far as I've been so far."

"Don't worry about the location of the bar. It isn't important." He took a big swig from the can. "We found we had a lot in common."

"Drinking, intrigue, women?" suggested Steve.

Macbride smiled. "Not necessarily in that order, but when he happened to ask me how many wives I'd had and I replied 'Do you mean of my own?' that sealed it between us. But there was something else. You probably don't know, in fact I'm sure you don't."

Steve showed more interest now; he had no knowledge of Macbride's past before the time they had been virtually thrown together in Central Africa ten years previously.

"I'm Scots Canadian," explained Macbride. "Grew up in Newfoundland in a tiny place called Greeleytown. It's not shown on large scale maps of the island but it's in the same area, the Avalon Peninsula, as St John's, the capital of the province. The crucial point of all this is that that was near where the early attempts at flying across the Atlantic took off. At school we learned about the early fliers and I dreamed of flying. So as soon as I was eighteen I joined the Royal Canadian Air Force and trained as a pilot. Three years later I moved to England, following a woman who didn't become my wife, and transferred to the RAF. Another three years and I got a special posting into a non-uniform group headed by Agnew. I've been there ever since, plenty of action but no active flying involved. However, my interest in aviation has never left me and that was the bond between me and Sergio as he was at that time a squadron commander in the Italian Air Force."

"So Janice was right thinking he was an Air Force man," said Steve.

"At that time yes, but then he moved into satellite surveillance."

"Ah, that's what the barman at Do Mori said."

"But it was our joint interest in aviation that brought us in contact. He let me tag along to a high-level international convention of plane designers and test pilots that was held in a very upmarket hotel on the island of San Clemente in the southern part of the lagoon. There was an asylum for the mentally deranged there until the late 1970s, but now there's the hotel, which the convention had taken over completely. Some sessions were very technical and others too politically sensitive for him to get a pass for me, so we only had a day and a half there, but it was enough to make some American contacts that would have made our friend

Brosnich green with envy. It also alerted me to the possibilities of the use of aerial drones that could be operated by pilots remote from the action."

"Surely they've been around for longer than that?" protested Steve.

"Yeah, but the problem is accuracy. The numbers of civilians killed by drone strikes in Afghanistan shows that, but those guys at the convention were talking about a new generation of drones that were at the drawing board stage which would have a pinpoint accuracy of three metres. That figure staggered me."

Steve looked from the door of the apartment to the window. "That's some accuracy. In the right hands they could be extremely useful. In the wrong hands..." He didn't bother to finish his comment.

Macbride nodded. "The other thing that struck me about it, though only after a few days, was that Sergio hadn't been surprised. He was obviously in the know. Then the next I heard about him after that visit was that he'd left the Air Force and was heading up the Veneto region department dealing with satellite surveillance."

"So you haven't met since?"

"Yes we have, about eight months ago, in Edinburgh of all places. Agnew put me on to it. Evidently through membership of NATO all the member countries are committed to a military alliance to provide common security and to co-operate and consult on scientific and other non-military fields. Satellite imagery has taken over from surveyors working on the ground and the data from that is shared between the countries, so now almost every square inch of ground in Europe is covered. And just to make sure everyone is totally involved they have an annual meeting of the regional heads."

"So eight months ago the meeting was in Edinburgh and Sergio was one of the regional heads?"

"Quick on the uptake as ever," said Macbride sarcastically, before draining his beer.

"If Hans Blix had been able to access that sort of data on Iraq then that conflict might never have started," mused Steve.

"It's only surface land-use that's revealed," explained Macbride. "So if there are underground silos they don't show up, but well-trained analysts can or should spot unusual activity."

"Perhaps Pinot's hideaway might be revealed," said Steve flippantly.

"Well, I'll see what Sergio has to offer on that score tomorrow. I'm off now to my luxury abode. We'll have a continental breakfast together, nine-thirty, at the next bar down from Janice's. I think we'll leave Janice as one of your contacts, at least for the moment."

"So you'll be chasing up Sergio and I'll..."

"Claudia Mancini for you my lad, but don't rush it. Remember, as far as we know, she was the last one Pinot had any contact with and for that to have happened there must have been earlier contacts. We need to know how, when, and why. Then the Adelaide bar for our lunch at one, or if I'm not there, back here by four."

Steve waited till he heard Macbride close the door to the street, then he moved to close the window. Macbride was striding along to the Tre Archi bridge – not the direction Steve had expected him to take, but this was not his first visit to the city.

Half an hour later Steve was back in Andrea's restaurant, but this time he decided to have a main course and a dessert, not just for the food but to have more opportunity to observe the other customers. He also found himself thinking about Macbride and Sergio, drones and surveillance. And then there was the prospect of meeting up with Claudia, the head turner.

CHAPTER 12

Steve had a restless night; the apartment seemed airless. At three o'clock he had had enough, so he left the tiny bedroom and went into the living room with the intention of opening the window onto the balcony. There was no need to switch on a light, as there was no cloud cover and the moonlight was sufficient for him to make his way round the furniture.

He was about to open it when the glow of a cigarette alerted him to an open boat moored on the far side of the canal. There were two men in the boat. Although he couldn't be completely sure, he didn't think the boat had been there when he had watched Macbride striding along towards the Tre Archi bridge a few hours earlier.

He abandoned the idea of opening the window and instead pulled the armchair around so it was facing the canal and settled down in it. He preferred to play the role of watcher rather than that of the one being watched.

At six o'clock the canal began to be busy and half an hour later the boat opposite started up its outboard and moved off in the direction of the lagoon. Both the men were aboard. Had they been watching him, perhaps to check if he had any visitors, or were they not interested in him at all? There might well be an innocent explanation, thought Steve but after the attack on Gianni less than twelve hours earlier, it seemed to him that his presence in the city and his enquiries about Pinot were causing concern in some quarters.

Just after eight Steve sauntered along to the Guglie bridge. He kept to the canal side, as he was moving against the main flow of people, which was made up of students making their way to the university buildings. They had an average age of around twenty, and he had a sudden pang of envy, but he reflected that their time would come when they made decisions that they might or might not regret. It brought to mind one of his father's favourite poems, 'The Road Not Taken' by Robert Frost:

Two roads diverged in a yellow wood
And sorry I could not travel both
And be one traveller, long I stood
And looked down one as far as I could
To where it bent in the undergrowth;

It ends:
I took the one less travelled by,
And that has made all the difference.

At the bridge he joined a much more varied crowd making their way down the Ria Terra San Leonardo. From a distance he could see that Janice's bar was doing good business. Not wanting to be involved with them, he kept himself to the further side of the pavement, but with the crush of people and Janice and her staff very busy in serving their customers, he need not have worried.

This also gave him the opportunity to check out the warehouse in the side street where Janice had suggested Pinot could store his artwork. It had a tall, wide, windowless door which was shut and secured with a heavy padlock, and there was no sign of anyone setting up an art stall in the area near Janice's bar which had been his pitch. It was much as he'd expected. He did think it might be an idea to get into the lock-up, although that would have to wait until after his breakfast with Macbride and, especially, after his meeting with the American woman.

Moving down to the next bar, just opposite the decorative façade of the Teatro Italia, he saw that Macbride was already seated at one of the shady outside tables. The empty cup in front of him indicated he had been there a while.

Steve took an adjoining chair and ordered a croissant and a double espresso for each of them from the nearest waiter. "You were up bright and early," he said.

Macbride nodded in an absent-minded fashion. "But not necessarily of my choice."

Nothing further was said until their order arrived. Steve curbed his impatience and waited. Obviously something was troubling Macbride, but he knew he wouldn't be rushed into an explanation. Macbride for his part was speculatively watching the passing crowd from under the brim of his hat. Occasionally he turned his head to watch a hip-swaying female and what looked like an approving smile crossed his features.

Eventually he turned back to face Steve. There was no trace of a smile now. "I've received some worrying news from Agnew," he said. "Came through less than half an hour ago. I presume he's been checking up on what Brosnich said to him yesterday."

"And it affects us?" said Steve.

"Yeah, but more immediately me. After I left you last night I caught up with Sergio at one of his favourite little drinking places. We only had an hour or so, just time for a few grappas. We talked of old times and drank to them; we talked of present times and the future and drank to them also. We were the buddies we had always been, honest and open with each other. Then, out of the blue, he suddenly remembered he had to move on to a special appointment, I suspect with a female. I said I'd call in to see him at his office this morning to finish our chat. So when you go off to make yourself known to Claudia, that's where I'll be."

"And the news from Agnew?" asked Steve.

"Four words only – 'Sergio may be suspect'. That's all."

Steve took his time in responding. Finally he asked, "While you were having your chat last night, did you happen to mention that an acquaintance of yours was in an apartment near the Tre Archi bridge? And after he left, do you think he'd have time to have the apartment watched?"

"Why?" growled Macbride, leaning across the table.

Steve told him about the two men he'd seen that night. Macbride eased himself back in his chair, allowing his gaze to follow a group of back-packers, most of them female, but his mind was on other things; he was thinking back to his conversation with Sergio.

"Fortunately, although I didn't have Agnew's warning then, when Sergio asked me where I was staying I just had a notion that I didn't want him to know about my rooming place. I just said I was bedding down temporarily in a place near the Tre Archi bridge and left it at that."

"And you're still going to meet up with him again?" asked Steve.

"Forewarned is forearmed. But don't ever let any of this get to the ears of Agnew," he added, twisting a fist against the heavy metal table rim. "However, I've got to give credit to Sergio, or whoever, because it was bloody quick work to get that organised."

"He's obviously no mug," replied Steve. "And he has contacts."

"If we link that to the stabbing of the Parlamento bloke you'd spoken to it looks pretty obvious that we are not particularly welcome here. The target could have been the restaurant, but I think we'll assume it could also be your apartment." Macbride leaned back in his chair and gazed up at the overhead canopy, deep in thought. "Sergio's no fool and he probably thinks he's ahead of us. I'll change my plans. Before I make my way to his work place I'll do a bit of delving at the office of an organisation called UK-Northern Italy Industry Links."

Steve raised his eyebrows. "And they are?"

"According to their literature, they are an organisation that makes it easy for big household name companies to trade, both here in Italy and back in the UK. For us it's also a useful front and Pinot's contact worked there."

"Pinot's late contact," corrected Steve.

Macbride nodded. "Yes, the late Charles Alsobri. While I'm doing that, you see if you can catch up with Claudia. We'll swap notes at your place at four or, if that's not on, then at six. Any later than that and we'll make it the Adelaide."

With that he pushed himself to his feet, threw his coat over his arm and walked out into the crowd. The waiter appeared as if he had expected this and presented the bill to Steve, who grimaced and paid. He stood and watched Macbride's heavily-built form strolling up the street through the passage the other pedestrians cleared for him. A man to be noticed and avoided, he thought.

Macbride made his way back to his room and checked the address and opening times of the Industry Links office. From his rooming place to the Marcuola traghetto crossing was less than five minutes, and it was the quickest way into the San Polo sestiere. From the traghetto landing point he made his way to the small campo of S. Giovanni Decollato. The Industry Links office was situated in the middle of a block facing the church, although it was not immediately obvious. The entrance was almost obscured by ill-tended, overgrown shrubs fighting for their existence in a small and heavily-shaded garden. That, and the fact that the business plaque on the door was difficult to read, gave the impression that they were not really seeking to encourage prospective clients. But Macbride was not a prospective client and, in any case, he was a man who was not easily discouraged.

He pushed the door open, stepped inside and found

himself in a different world; plush carpets, panelled walls and the very faint hum of an air conditioning unit.

"Can I be of assistance, sir?" a voice said from the open door of an office. It was followed by its owner, a small, elderly man dressed most elegantly in a dark grey business suit.

"I'm not sure if I'm in the right place," answered Macbride, with a backward glance to the unkempt garden. "I'm from London," he added. "It's about Mr Alsobri."

The man nodded. "You're in the right place. We don't have as many personal callers as we once did, because most of our business is now done via the internet. It was only this morning that we were told to expect you. I'm Parsons, head of the office here."

He extended his hand and Macbride shook it. "You have a strong grip," said Macbride.

"In my younger days I rowed competitively, now just for pleasure," Parsons said, a touch of pride in his voice. Then, as he remembered the reason for Macbride's visit, he added, "We were all devastated by Charlie's death."

"Very sad," agreed Macbride. "A hit and run, we were told."

"A terrible accident. Must have been. Charlie had only been with us a year and was a very quiet man. A loner, some would say, but I never heard a bad word said about him. He loved nothing better than to go off on his bike when he had any free time. He was also keen on photography. The bike and his photography – they were his passions."

"Was he any good as a photographer?"

"I think he must have been. A couple of times last month a man came to see him here and Charlie said it was about his photos and that he might be entering some in a competition."

"So he must have been pretty good. Did he mention the name of the competition?"

"No. As I said, Charlie was a very quiet young man."

"And the man?" asked Macbride.

"I never saw him. I had an important client here and it was Charlie's affair, so I didn't have any words with him. I have enough to do running the business. Adele, my secretary, saw him and passed him on to Charlie."

They were both silent for a few moments, then Parsons clapped his hands together. "My goodness," he said. "Where have my manners gone? Come into the office and I'll have coffee sent in to us."

The office was spacious and beautifully furnished, without a book, folder or paper spoiling the tidiness of Parsons' desk. Macbride thought that either he was ultra-efficient in his work or the business was not overtaxing. A young woman, smartly dressed, brought in a tray with coffee and some fancy pastries, placed them on a side table, then left them. Mr Parsons poured the coffee and while they drank and ate they engaged in small talk.

Macbride didn't want to rush things; there might still be things to learn or confirm.

"I understand you are seeing to the funeral arrangements."

"Yes, Charlie had no living relatives so London have asked me to do it," replied Parsons.

"What about personal effects?"

"He was a practising Catholic, so I'll be turning everything over to them. I think that's best, don't you?"

"You're probably right, but there might be some things that could be of interest to us," said Macbride. "Letters, or some of his photographs?"

"Now you mention it, there is a notebook. It's in his office drawer. I thought it had to do with his photography. I'll get it for you now," said Parsons, jumping to his feet, obviously keen to start the process of disposing of Charlie's effects.

He was gone for longer than Macbride had expected and when he returned he was shaking his head. "It's not there, yet I'm sure it was three days ago."

"One of your staff or a cleaner perhaps could have moved it?" suggested Macbride.

"No. They were told not to touch anything of his."

"No visitors?"

"No. At least only the chap I mentioned to you before. He was here a couple of days ago, but I was out. I was told he waited for a while but then said he couldn't wait any longer."

"You still can't remember his name?"

Parsons cupped his chin in his left hand and his brow furrowed. "Adele may have caught it." He called for her and the young woman who'd brought in the coffee reappeared.

"Do you know the name of the man who came the other day to see Charlie about his photographs?" he asked her.

Adele wrinkled her brow in an effort to remember. "Oh, it was something like Silvio, or was it Stefano?" Then, after a further moment's thought, she shook her head. "No, I'm sorry. I think I'd just be guessing."

"Don't worry about it," said Parsons. He waved his hand and Adele left the room.

"If it does come back to her or the notebook surfaces, let

the London office know," said Macbride. "They'll pass the information on to me."

Parsons readily agreed, and Macbride took his leave. He had no answers, but he had learned that someone had met Alsobri, Pinot's contact, shortly before his fatal crash, and had then been back to the office and, presumably, taken a notebook from his desk drawer. It was beginning to look as though that person might also be trying to find Pinot or to find out what Pinot knew. Somehow he – and Steve – would have to get ahead of him.

He decided to postpone his meeting with Sergio until the following day to give himself more time to sort out his thoughts, and also to hear if Steve had contacted Claudia. On the way back to his room he called at Sergio's office near the Rialto bridge and left a note at reception. Rather than waste the afternoon, he reckoned he might be better off checking the Do Mori area in the hope that some of the others in Pinot's and Sergio's wandering group might be there. More information, especially from a third party, might be revealing.

He used his fairly limited Italian to ask several local people for directions, and twenty minutes later, he was in the Do Mori bar. The place was very quiet. The casual morning drinkers and the local tradespeople having a light lunch had all passed through.

The barman was happy to chat, but when he was asked if Pinot or Sergio had been there that day he said neither had been there for at least a week as far as he knew, although he only worked there every other day. Macbride was disappointed. But as he was about to leave, the barman said, "The person who might be able to help you is an

American woman who lives in Venice for about four months every year. She's been coming here for about fifteen years; she seems to latch on to a different, rich Italian every year in this area. She's quite attractive, in a buxom way, and for a couple of glasses of vino she'll give you her life story. And she's a very pleasant, helpful person."

"Do you know her name and where I could find her?" asked Macbride.

"Her name is Marlene, and you'll find her anywhere in the bar area around here. Try the second street up from here; there's a very small place where I think she has lunch. She might still be there."

Macbride thanked him, downed his glass of wine and set off in search of Marlene. His luck was in. At the entrance to the bar that had been suggested to him, an attractive, buxom woman was about to leave.

"Are you Marlene?" he asked.

"Who's asking, dear?" She had a pleasant, educated, American accent.

"I'm William Johnson, Bill to my friends back in England. I'm trying to locate a couple of friends from way back."

"Very pleased to make your acquaintance, Bill. I like the English, especially mature English men. Perhaps we could have a drink and see if I know these friends of yours?"

"That would be most kind of you," said Macbride, doing his best impression of a mature Englishman.

Inside the tiny bar there was an empty table immediately behind the door, ideal for a quiet chat. Macbride ordered a carafe of red wine and two glasses and paid as soon as they arrived. He poured the wine.

"And who are these two friends of yours, Bill?" asked Marlene.

"One is a half-English, half-Hungarian man called Pinot. The other is an Italian called Sergio."

She took a sip of her wine. "I know them both," she said. "Pinot only slightly, Sergio a little better."

Macbride couldn't help but notice the wistfulness in her voice when she mentioned Sergio.

"You knew Sergio well?" asked Macbride.

"We were very close friends for several months," she said. "Then for no reason, at least no reason apparent to me, he started avoiding me. I decided to have it out with him, you know, clear the air." Macbride nodded, but made no reply. "So I went down to the place near his office and I saw him talking to a group of men that, for want of a better word, I could only describe as thugs. They were not the sort I would want to be associated with."

"And was Sergio arguing with them?"

"No. He seemed to be giving them orders and they were all nodding. I was a little distance away, but it looked like they were his men."

"Have you seen them again?" asked Macbride.

"No, and I certainly don't want to. Why Sergio should be involved with them is beyond me."

"Well if that's the way things are, thanks for the warning."

For the next twenty minutes they drank the wine and chatted, while Macbride steered the conversation away from the search.

"I'm leaving for the States in ten days' time," she said. "Back to my Florida husband, but I'll be back in Venice again next spring. If you're here we could meet up."

"That's an interesting proposition," said Macbride, pushing himself to his feet.

Marlene looked up at him. "Your name isn't Bill Johnson, is it?"

Macbride bent down and brushed the backs of his fingers against her cheek, then softly kissed it. "Let's see what next year brings," he said.

"That thought will keep me going through the winter. Bye Bill."

Macbride made his way across to the other side of the Grand Canal. He had the feeling that some things were beginning to fall into place.

CHAPTER 13

Steve made his way in the opposite direction from that taken by Macbride. The narrow Calle di Ca' d'Oro took him past the side entrance to the Franchetti Museum and led him to the vaporetto stop on the Grand Canal. A single journey across the canal took him to the stop for the Rialto Mercato. He was very much looking forward to meeting Claudia the head turner. All in the interests of work, he reminded himself, and smiled. He also remembered that although she would already have been told of his presence in the city, he had to make their meeting appear casual.

At the vaporetto stop most of the other passengers who were leaving the boat seemed to be locals, as they were carrying shopping bags and almost all of them went through the arch, turned right, and determinedly made their way along to the vegetable and fish markets. Steve moved into a doorway set into the archway out of the main flow of people, pulled out the city map he'd brought from the apartment and sorted out his route to the Ruga Vecchia, where Claudia had her morning coffee. A uniformed security man was making his way down the stone stairway, presumably from an upstairs office, but Steve moved on. His route could hardly have been more straightforward; no bridges over small canals or twisting calli to negotiate.

Directly in front of the archway was a small square with a caffeteria's outside tables and chairs and in the right-hand corner was the entrance to the Ruga San Giovanni, which led into the Ruga Vecchia. The easy part, he thought; now it's just a question of meeting up with her.

No sooner had that thought crossed his mind when he saw, on the far side of the square, a woman who seemed to match the description he had been given. She was tall, slim and stylishly dressed with dark, shoulder-length hair, and she was carrying a light brown executive-style briefcase. She was looking in the window of an art shop. After checking her watch, she went into the shop.

Quickly Steve made his way across. First he spent a moment looking, quite intently, at the watercolours on display in the window, and then he shifted his gaze to the inside of the tiny shop. A young man was seated in front of an easel with a partially-finished painting on it. As soon as he saw the woman, he stood up. They kissed on both cheeks and began to chat; they were obviously friends. Now that he was able to have a closer look at her, Steve hoped that it was Claudia; she was certainly a head-turner.

Just at that moment she suddenly moved across to the window display and pointed out a particular painting to the artist, who carefully lifted it out to allow her to see it more closely. It was then that she saw Steve. She showed just the merest hint of recognition and surprise before she turned back to examine the painting.

Steve had already given her top marks for her looks, and now he had to add to that his admiration for her composure. Claudia was something special.

He waited a moment before entering the shop. The two of them were talking animatedly in rapid Italian, obviously discussing the painting. Claudia made the slightest of gestures to the artist and then turned to face Steve.

"I hope you weren't considering buying this," she said in faultless English. "Nicola and I have just this morning agreed a price." Then over her shoulder she spoke again in Italian and Nicola took the painting into the back area of the shop, which was curtained off from the rest of his work area. For a few minutes they were alone. Steve looked around at the work on display, which ranged from small calendar wallets of local scenes to much more ambitious works similar to the one Claudia was buying.

"He's probably the best artist working in the Veneto area today," Claudia said, just as Nicola reappeared. He laughed. "How can I fail to be a success when I'm given such a glowing reference?" he said in good English.

"Well deserved, and you know it," responded Claudia. "If you would send it over to the Gritti Palace next Wednesday that would be ideal," she added as she moved to the door.

"No problem," said Nicola, "and thank you again."

"Well I'm here for a week or more, so I'll certainly be back," said Steve over his shoulder. He held the door open then, with a rather self- conscious "*Ciao*," he followed

Claudia outside. She strolled along in the direction of the Rialto, but instead of keeping to the main thoroughfare she turned into the narrow walkway which ran behind the shops. Steve followed and she allowed him to catch up.

Without stopping she said, "You're from England and you are called what?"

"Cromarty, Steve Cromarty," he answered, "And you're from Marano?"

"Claudia Mancini. I believe I have met someone you know. What is his name again?"

"I think you'd know him as Pinot," said Steve.

She nodded. "We understand each other."

"I think you can help me and Pinot. But we need to have a talk."

"My work needs me this morning," she answered, "but I should be free by one o'clock and I intend to have lunch at the Leon Bianco."

"I would join you if I knew where it was," replied Steve.

"You have a map?"

"Do you think I would have been allowed out without one?"

"Campo Manin," she said. "I'll meet you there. To find it, cross the Rialto, go through Campo San Bartolomeo, then past the big church of San Salvatore and into Campo San Luca. The next square is the Campo Manin with its statue of Manin. If you forget the names just ask for the Manin."

"I'll be there mooching around at one," answered Steve.

"Good, but will you recognize me?" she asked.

"Five seven, twelve stone, large feet. Who wouldn't?" he quipped.

She smiled, and her eyes sparkled. "See you," she said.

Then she turned abruptly and made her way past sacks of various spices into the back entrance of a shop.

Steve walked on and rejoined the main route to the double flight of stone steps which led up to the bridge. Looking at his watch, he saw that he had just over three hours before his lunch with Claudia. He stood on the main level of the bridge, idly looking down at the water traffic without really taking in the scene. Finding Pinot was an urgent matter and he didn't want to waste the next three hours. Breaking into Pinot's art store would be best done in late evening with Macbride, but checking out other artists working for the tourist trade could be done now and might yield something useful. At least it was a course of action, better than wandering around aimlessly.

On the far side of the bridge he used a five-euro note to catch the interest of an under-employed young waiter standing outside a pizzeria.

"Where's the best place to find artists selling their work outside on the streets?" he asked.

"There are a few around here, but many more near St Mark's," the waiter replied.

"Thanks," said Steve.

"No problem, sir. And if you don't find what you want, there's a very clever man outside Accademia."

Steve pushed another note into the man's hand. "Thanks, and which is the best way to reach St Mark's?"

The man pointed to the nearest vaporetto stop. "Take the number one boat which is going out to the Lido, but you get off at San Marco Vallaresso. It's eight stops from here."

The Number 1 boat, when it arrived, looked as though it already had its full quota of passengers, but Steve was among about thirty others who managed to squeeze aboard. The morning was turning out well. The waiter's directions were faultless and from the Vallaresso stop, along a shrub-lined pavement, there were half a dozen artists showing works for sale. However, when he tried to engage them in conversation they were not interested; they were there to sell, not talk.

He moved on towards two stone columns, one with a winged lion on top, the other with an odd-looking crocodile, which seemed to be guarding the seaward entrance to the main square of the city, the Piazza San Marco. To his right was the famous Doge's Palace, but he saw no artists working there, so he walked past the towering brick-built bell tower into the huge square, which was bounded on three sides by massive stone buildings with colonnaded walkways. The fourth side was completely dominated by the ancient basilica. For a few minutes Steve forgot his reason for being there; surely no one could fail to be impressed by the combination of beauty, wealth and power on display here. The huge Byzantine domes, rearing horses over the massive door, gold and mosaic facades, were much more impressive in reality than in any tourist bumph he'd seen.

But there was work to be done. In the central part of the square there were more artists at work, all of them keen to talk to tourists who might be willing to part with large wads of cash. Steve didn't come into that category, so he spent a fruitless half-hour wandering along the row, until he reluctantly had to admit he was wasting his time.

He decided to make his way to the Accademia to try his luck there. The 'very clever man', as the waiter had intriguingly called him, might have had some sort of rapport with Pinot, who, Steve had to grudgingly admit to himself, was also a very clever man. The vaporetto journey to the Accademia bridge was quicker, only three stops, and much more pleasant, as at that time in the morning there were fewer tourists coming back from, rather than going to, the Lido. Standing on the almost empty outer deck, Steve was able to get a fine view of the huge Salute church as the vessel pulled into the stop there, then further on the low building, which he'd missed on the way down the canal, with its banner proclaiming to the world that it housed the Peggy Guggenheim collection of modern art.

The Accademia was his destination and the boat nosed its way under the heavy-looking wooden bridge to the floating pontoons. As he stepped onto the solid pavement he was very conscious of the contrast between the broad canal with its open sky and the cramped, cluttered, shadowed area he was now standing in. It was caused by the combination of the solid bulk of the Accademia building, the dark wooden bridge supports and a magazine vendor's kiosk. It didn't seem a likely place for an artist to successfully persuade tourists to part with money.

However, he couldn't have been more wrong. Tucked into a sheltered, overhanging corner of the building an elderly artist was working, and he had attracted a good number of people. Steve stood at the back of the crowd and watched. He was amazed by the skill of the man and by his unusual method. He was working with sticks of charcoal in such a way that he seemed to be able to recreate broad strokes, fine straight lines and curved lines until, before the eyes of the watchers, a Venetian scene emerged on the white sheet of paper. And all of this was done without looking at an actual scene or a photograph.

He had to stop several times to attend to people who were anxious to buy his work. Steve noted that although several nationalities were involved, the artist spoke to many of them in their own language. So he was multi-lingual. Steve could well imagine Pinot being a friend of this man.

While the transactions were taking place one of the crowd asked the question on everyone's lips: "Where have these images come from?"

The artist put down his charcoal and tapped the side of his temple. "I am Venetian. I have lived here all my life. More than eighty per cent of Venice is locked in my brain and I can reproduce it purely by concentrating." He spoke with a heavy accent, but his English was good. He smiled around at them all, then continued, "But I also have to eat and my lunch will be waiting for me. If you are interested I'll be back here in an hour."

He started to pack up his various boxes and the crowd drifted away. Steve waited until the others had gone and the artist had picked up his boxes and folding chair and was about to take them to the magazine kiosk before he spoke.

"I have a friend who is an artist in the Cannareggio area," he said. "His name is Pinot. Do you know him?"

The artist stopped in his tracks and looked closely at Steve. "I do know a Pinot," he answered cautiously. "Despite his name, he is an Englishman. A very clever man. An interesting man."

"That sounds like my friend," said Steve. "Unfortunately we've lost touch and I'm trying to find him."

"Wait here till I put these things in the kiosk."

Steve nodded and waited. In a few minutes the artist returned with a worried look on his face.

"I am Rosario. Pinot and I are good friends; we have much in common. We only meet about once or twice every month or so, but I have heard that there are others, not Englishmen, who are also trying to find him. It is very worrying."

"You say you have much in common?"

"We cannot talk here," broke in Rosario. "Tomorrow I don't work. At ten thirty I will be in the Castello sestiere looking at Garibaldi's monument. Follow me from there to an apartment owned by my cousin, Beppe." He then quickly walked away around the corner of the art gallery.

Steve looked at his watch. He had forty minutes to make his way to Campo Manin and meet up with Claudia. He decided to walk, which meant ignoring the route she'd proposed. But he had a map and he felt buoyed with the results of his morning so far. He hoped Macbride was making similar progress.

He crossed the bridge, stopping only to read some of the messages of undying love which were written on the small padlocks that young people – he assumed they were young – had locked onto the bridge's wooden railings. Crossing the Campo San Vidal, he felt the heat of the day reflecting from all sides, and a cooling drink seemed like a good idea. Seeing nothing that appealed there, he made his way into the larger Campo Santo Stefano and found a shaded and well-patronised seating area. From the extensive list of drinks he chose a *frappucino.*

He had time to relax and enjoy it as he watched the general mix of tourists and locals, some with their dogs, and youngsters playing a strenuous game of football in the far corner of the square. At one point the ball was kicked against the far wall and bounced towards the tables, prompting a large dog to pull violently on its lead in an attempt to join in the game.

Steve finished his drink, checked his map, paid the bill and strolled along to the Campo Manin, which Claudia had mentioned. In the middle of it stood an impressive bronze statue of a man, and on the steps of the pedestal lay a bronze winged lion.

He was edging his way around looking for an explanatory plaque when Claudia appeared on the far side of the statue, her light blue dress accentuating the curves of her body. Steve lost interest in the statue and moved towards her. The blue of the dress matched the colour of her eyes, which sparkled with recognition as she saw him. The light breeze blew her dark wavy hair back from her face. She looked cool, confident and happy.

Steve gave her his most winning smile. She returned the smile and then gestured at the statue.

"He's Daniele Manin," she said, nodding towards him. "A famous Venetian revolutionary. He was the first and only President of the Republic of San Marco. But I assume you would rather have lunch than a history lesson."

She took his arm and led him out of the square past the modern concrete and glass frontage of a bank into the Salizada San Luca, where the Osteria Leon Bianco was situated.

"I think I could have found it," said Steve, putting his hand over hers.

She smiled, then, taking her arm away, she said, "We're here. Just follow me and do the same as me. It's a kind of self-service."

Steve obeyed, and Claudia ordered food for the two of them at the counter; plates of lasagne with bean salad and two glasses of *vino rosso della casa.* The inner area of the trattoria was a canvas marquee, and Claudia chose a table there. They returned to the counter, collected their food and carried it back to their table.

"A very efficient system," said Steve approvingly. "And I presume the wage bill will be fairly low."

"Yes. The food is very good, nothing fancy, and probably because there's no waiter service, the prices are very reasonable. The customers are all people who work round here and that's how they like it."

As they ate Steve glanced around. The other customers looked like office workers, mainly men, and at the furthest end were two members of the local police force, who didn't appear to be eating quite as hurriedly as the rest. It was the same the world over, he reflected.

Claudia and Steve ate in silence and it was only when they were sipping the wine that Steve broached the subject of Pinot and how Claudia knew him.

"I've known him for about a year. Our paths crossed, purely by chance, when we both happened to be making enquiries about certain individuals who were suspected of people smuggling. When I mentioned him to my superior…"

"Brosnich?" said Steve.

She nodded. "Yes," she said. "He asked me many questions about him. Eventually, he said he was sure he knew him, but not by the name of Pinot. He told me that at some time Pinot might be of some use to us, so I wasn't warned off but I had to take extreme care."

"So did you meet regularly?"

"Oh no, that could have compromised us both. But we did know where we could find each other." Steve raised his eyebrows. "Between Nicola's art shop, where we were this morning, and the Rialto Bridge is the Campo San Giacomo. In the corner of it there is a stone carving of a crouching hunchback. If Pinot needed to communicate he would be there at ten in the morning on a Wednesday or Friday. I always checked it out on those days."

"And if he was there?" asked Steve.

"Our arrangement was that I would make my way into the church at the Rialto end of the square, the San Giacomo di Rialto. It's the one with the huge twenty-four-hour clock outside. And he would follow me in."

"And how many times did this sort of meeting take place?"

"Just the once," she answered. "Ten days ago. He was very agitated, not behaving at all as you'd expect. He kept saying 'I've got to get out, I've got to get out'. I said 'What about your contact?' He just shook his head and said 'He seems to have disappeared. I can't hang around, they're after me'. Then he grabbed my arm briefly and said, 'Get a message out if you can,' and almost ran out of the church."

"And you informed Brosnich, who passed it to London?"

"Yes."

"And you haven't seen Pinot since and you don't know what his problem was?"

"No, but I can assure you he was a very frightened man."

Steve swirled his wine round in the glass, apparently

lost in thought. Then he abruptly changed the subject. "Do you have any dealings with an ex-military man called Sergio?"

Claudia rose to her feet. "Too quickly, too far, Steve," she said. "I'll need to get clearance."

Steve, who had watched other diners pick up their plates and glasses and place them on a bare table at the end of the room, cleared the remains of their lunch and followed Claudia out into the street. She was waiting for him.

"You know it's not personal," she said.

"I've no problem with it," he answered. "Assuming you get the OK, where could we meet again?"

She pursed her lips as she considered the question. Then she looked directly at him and smiled.

"I don't normally come into Venice on a Saturday, but I could make an exception. It will also give me time to contact Brosnich and hopefully get clearance."

"Give me the time and the vaporetto stop and I'll be there," said Steve. "I have my trusty map," he added, tapping his coat pocket.

"Steve, in Venice I never use public transport, only the hotels' water taxis with known drivers. They are only allowed to use particular boarding points, not vaporetto stops, so probably the easiest for you to find would be on the Grand Canal at the side of the San Marcuola church. There are two vaporetto stops there, one for going down the canal and the other going up. They are about thirty yards apart and the jetty for launches is roughly midway between the two. Use your trusty map and be there at ten on Saturday."

She didn't wait for an answer.

CHAPTER 14

At ten minutes to four Steve was back in his apartment. He went through the same procedure as before to prepare himself for Macbride's arrival, except that he did not bother to have any beer cans ready. Having checked that the mooring opposite was empty, he spread his city map on the table and carefully traced his finger along the route he had followed since he left the apartment that morning. He felt he was now beginning to find his bearings, although Pinot was proving to be elusive.

Tomorrow's arrangements would take him into the Castello sestiere, the centre of the ancient shipbuilding area, and a quick search of that section of the map showed him that he should have no problem in locating the Monumento a Garibaldi, where he was to meet up with Rosario.

Then he remembered that that was not quite true – Rosario had not said he would meet up with him. He had specifically said that he would be waiting at the monument at ten-thirty and that Steve would have to follow him from there to his cousin's apartment. Obviously Rosario, although a friend of Pinot's, did not want to be seen meeting up with someone who was seeking to find his friend. It seemed the 'undesirables' that Gianni had mentioned had cast a wider net.

Just as he was pondering this, he became aware of a small boat slowly nudging its way along the far side of the canal. There was only one man on board, but within a minute of tying up to the same mooring the boat of the previous night had used, he was joined by a second. If they had been wearing police uniforms they could have been easily mistaken for the two *carabinieri* who had been idly enjoying their lunch in the Leon Bianco at the same time as he and Claudia.

As Steve watched, he became aware that the sky had taken on a sullen, darkening hue and then in minutes the surface of the canal was pitted with large, heavy raindrops. The two men on the boat hurriedly began to pull a large tarpaulin over themselves.

Along the broad pavement area, a group of people who had been making a leisurely way towards the Tre Archi bridge had been caught unawares by the suddenness of the storm. They were now huddled against the buildings and attempting to gain some shelter while they struggled into rainwear. Some were attempting to open out umbrellas, but they quickly realised that this was futile, as a strong wind had sprung up and was funnelling down the canal from the lagoon.

As they continued on their way, almost bent double against the wind, a man detached himself from the far side of the group. Although the visibility through the heavy rain wasn't good, Steve was in no doubt that it was Macbride.

In the time it took Macbride to make his way round to the Tre Archi bridge and then reach the apartment, the storm had ended, almost as abruptly as it had begun. Steve helped himself to a can of beer; he decided he would have a drink while listening to Macbride. He settled himself in the chair to await his arrival.

"My god, you haven't just swum here have you?" he asked as the door was pushed open and a bedraggled Macbride appeared. Then, more seriously, he added, nodding at the canal, "They're back."

"Yeah, I saw them, and I don't think they're there for the good of their health. You're probably right. They're watching the apartment. They must have been put there by Sergio."

"And why should he be doing that?" Steve asked.

"That's what we need to know," answered a solemn Macbride. "It looks as though he's involved in some sort of strange game. But for us, forewarned is forearmed."

Steve mulled this over, then asked, "In your chat with him over your drinks he did admit to knowing Pinot, didn't he?"

"Oh yes, he had no problems with that. Spoke highly of him. He knows him as an interesting, intelligent man who manages to make a living of sorts by selling his paintings to tourists. He actually said he was the one who invited him to join the group who stroll around chatting and having drinks in the bars around the Rialto market areas. All of which I think he knew I was aware of. But when I suggested that in some way it was possible Pinot might have been involved in information gathering, he laughed out loud."

"And that may be the point where honesty failed him, even to you," said Steve.

Macbride nodded. "Sergio I like. Agnew I trust." Then he abruptly changed the subject. "And your day – useful I hope?"

Steve gave a detailed account of his meetings with Claudia and Rosario. Macbride listened intently. A sudden flash of lightning illuminated the room, followed very quickly by a tremendous crash of thunder. Then the rain began again in earnest.

"I think the gods are trying to tell us something," said Macbride. "It's just the night we need to have a look in the lock-up store Pinot uses for his artwork."

"True, this storm will even drive the rats off the streets," agreed Steve. "But we don't have any keys. Janice did mention that she has a spare so that one of her lads could push Pinot's stuff back in if he wasn't back to do it himself by the time they shut the bar up, but that's never been necessary."

"I don't want to involve Janice in any of this," answered Macbride. "I know a hardware place where I can get a bolt cutter and a new padlock. I'll see to that. So see if you can find me a hat and I'll be off. We'll meet up again at Janice's corner at ten-thirty. That'll give you time to eat at Andrea's place."

A quick search of the apartment resulted only in the

finding of an old dark brown rubberised coat. “It'll do. You're not in a fashion show,” said Steve, but he was talking to himself, as Macbride was already down to the first landing.

Steve left the restaurant at ten-twenty. The storm had abated, but it was a very dark evening with a particular heaviness in the air which suggested that more rain was still possible. He saw only two people on his way to the meeting place. Both were dog walkers who were out only as a matter of duty to their canine pets, and that was where their attention was focused.

Macbride was standing in a recessed doorway. Together they moved down the street to Pinot's lock-up. Although the padlock was strong it yielded to the heavy-duty bolt cutters that Macbride had brought. Pulling one of the doors open they entered the store, then carefully closed the door behind them before Steve switched on his torch.

The warehouse was surprisingly spacious, with ample room for the large four-wheeled trolley which stood in the centre. Several large completed paintings were stacked on it. To Steve's eye they were as good, if not better, than most of the ones he had seen that morning, apart from those done by Nicola, Claudia's friend, and Rosario's charcoal sketches. Grudgingly he had to agree with the view expressed by several that Pinot was ‘a clever man, an interesting man’, yet they knew nothing of his other life.

Along one side of the room there was a long bench which held a number of works which were at various stages of completion, along with brushes and tubes of paint carefully arranged. At the back, almost hidden by the trolley, there was a desk and chair and on the desk were some large playing cards. There appeared to be three sets of them, all showing the same pattern. Macbride picked up one of the sets, turned the cards over and took the torch from Steve.

"There are some numbers here, on the back of one of them," he said. "Written in pencil, but very faint and hard to make out." He made a note of the numbers on a sheet of paper lying on the desk, put it in his pocket, and handed the torch back. "Probably of no significance," he said, "But you never know."

They then moved to the other side of the room and Steve swung the beam of the torch round. Here there were more canvases, but, of more interest to them, there was a door in the wall and a couple of yards from it an open wooden staircase which led up to a mezzanine area.

Macbride tried the door; it was locked. Steve examined the lock. "I presume this leads out to an alley. If we'd known we could have picked this and saved ourselves some trouble."

"Mm," grunted Macbride. "Let's see what's up here." He started up the stairs, and Steve followed. The torch lit up the contents; a camp bed which looked as though it had been used recently, a small table and a shelf unit with an assortment of tinned food and several bottles of water.

"Obviously not a permanent residence," said Steve. "It's either a place he used if he was working late on one of his paintings and couldn't be bothered to go home, or it was a bolt hole."

Macbride nodded his agreement. "Let's check where that door leads," he said, and they made their way back down the stairs.

From the inside, the lock was no problem. They carefully looked out into a short and very narrow passageway. There was no light other than that which filtered into it from the street which ran along from Janice's bar. They made their way back into the warehouse and locked the door.

"What do you make of it?" asked Steve.

"It's a bolt hole, and he's used it very recently I reckon," answered Macbride. "I'm hoping if he tries to use it again he'll use that side door, because I'll have to put the new padlock on the front when we leave."

It was just after eleven when they closed the warehouse door and secured it. The rain was just beginning again as they went their separate ways.

"I'll phone you early," was Macbride's parting promise.

CHAPTER 15

Steve slept only fitfully, partly due to the ferocity of the storm, which lasted through the greater part of the night, and partly because his brain would not stop bringing up images of Pinot's art store and bolthole. He woke with two nagging questions: when had Pinot last been there? And was there any significance in the numbers that Macbride had found on one of the playing cards?

When dawn broke, the storm had cleared, and as Steve opened the balcony window a cool, fresh breath of air filled his lungs. Looking down on the canal, he saw that the boat containing the two watchers had gone. He then spent some time watching the early barges pass by and seeing the area gradually come to life.

His mobile phone rang. It was Macbride.

"Good, I hoped I'd catch you in. I want to bring you up

to date but not over the phone. I'll be on the Tre Archi bridge in a quarter of an hour."

Steve had showered and dressed by the time Macbride was making his way up the steps of the bridge from the Ghetto side of the canal. Two minutes later Steve had joined him.

"Does this mean the apartment isn't secure?" he asked.

"Now we know it's being watched it might not be," Macbride began, "but to make sure we'll be on the safe side. It's just you I want to put in the picture, not others."

He turned to lead the way back to the Fondamenta di Cannareggio and began walking along it towards the Guglie bridge before continuing.

"I don't think we should be too negative, Steve. I didn't expect Pinot to be sitting there waiting for us to turn up last night, but from what I saw I think he's still at large. We just have to find him."

"That's exactly where we were a few days ago," said Steve.

"No, I think you're being too pessimistic."

"Enlighten me."

"Well, I've had very little sleep since I last saw you."

"Me too," said Steve. "That was certainly a belter of a storm."

Macbride gave him a withering look. "Storms don't bother me," he replied.

"No," he added. "Remember the playing cards on the table?"

"I can see them now," said Steve. "All carefully arranged."

Macbride smiled. "Great minds, eh? But if you

remember, I made a note of some numbers that I could just make out on the back of one of them."

"And?"

They were now within yards of the pasticceria near the bridge. "First we'll have a coffee here," Macbride answered. They took their coffees to an inside table.

"And what thoughts have you had about them?" prompted Steve again.

"It struck me that the casino might provide a clue," Macbride answered, "so I rang Sergio and asked him…"

"You what?" broke in Steve. "You asked Sergio, after Agnew's warning?"

"Don't worry, lad. I explained why I'd called off yesterday's visit and only suggested a few hours at the casino. Sergio and I have had a few good long nights there in the past so I reckoned he'd be up for it. We were there till gone four, having a good time, chatting about this and that, and winning some and losing some."

"And the numbers on the card. Did they figure in any of this?" asked Steve.

"Unfortunately, no. But that's one more possibility discounted, so we just have to keep on looking. And, on the positive side, Sergio and I are getting on very well. He might still be useful to us."

"To you, maybe," said Steve, "but when I mentioned his name to Claudia yesterday she reacted like the proverbial cat on a hot tin roof. Said she'd have to get clearance before we can go further. Does that mean he has some link with Brosnich?"

"That I don't know, as yet. It's a possibility. Sergio's a really smart guy and he's certainly in the sort of position which would interest Brosnich. If your Claudia gets clearance then Monday might provide us with some answers."

"True," agreed Steve. "But in the meantime, today I've got a meeting lined up in Rosario's cousin's apartment in the Castello area."

"And I'm going to have another chat with Parsons at UK-Northern Italy Industry Links, just in case he's remembered something, anything, that might be of use to us."

"And time is pressing," said Steve.

"I don't need to be reminded," answered Macbride sourly. "Pinot would only have surfaced if he was on to something big and urgent. He surfaced on June 21st and it's now June 27th. I reckon we probably have days rather than weeks to get to the bottom of this. After that it'll probably be too late." He drained his coffee, then added, "But pessimism will not help anybody. Remember, hard work brings its own luck. We'll crack this one, Steve."

Before Macbride left the premises, Steve checked their arrangements for meeting that evening.

"As before. Adelaide, hourly, six till ten, or tomorrow morning breakfast at Janice's bar," said Macbride. And again, "We will crack it, Steve."

* * *

After Macbride had left the pasticceria, Steve ordered another espresso. It was just before seven-thirty, three hours before he was due to be in the area of the Garibaldi monument. The café was beginning to fill up with locals grabbing their shots of caffeine before going on their way to work. It was a jostling crowd, obviously well known to each other but exchanging only brief greetings, no real conversations developing. To Steve it looked as though their working day had in some ways already started. That thought jolted him; If Macbride was right in his assessment of the time available to them, he couldn't allow three hours to be wasted.

He steered his way past the customers standing at the bar and joined the early morning tourists heading in the direction of the Strada Nova. In ten minutes he was approaching Janice's bar, the place which he had decided should be his next port of call. What useful information he might glean from a further chat with her he wasn't sure, but it might not be wasted time.

He needn't have worried about how he would again raise the issue of Pinot with her as Janice, who seemed to have been looking out for him, hurried from the doorway of the café and grabbed him by the arm.

"I'm pleased you're here," she began. "Something happened at Pinot's storage place last night." Steve feigned ignorance, but expressed his interest.

"What sort of thing?" he asked.

"This isn't the best place for us to talk," she said, pulling him into the café and then into a room behind the serving area. "This morning two *agente di polizia finanze* were waiting here for me when I came to open up. They said they knew I had a key to the warehouse and they waved an official paper at me which they said authorised them to search the premises. I gave them the key, but they were back in a very short time and said the padlock had been changed and what did I know about it."

"And you knew nothing," said Steve.

"That's right. Nothing at all."

"So how did they react to that?"

"They left straight away. And when I had time to think about it, that seemed strange. I wondered if it was because customers were beginning to arrive."

"You're sure they were genuine?" said Steve.

Janice gave him a world-weary smile. "Steve, when you're in business in Venice and the finance police call on you, the last thing you do is get on the wrong side of them by querying their authority."

Steve nodded. He had more than a little sympathy with that view.

"By the way, did you catch up with Sergio?" she asked.

"Not yet," he answered. He decided to make no mention of Macbride's meeting.

"Well I could tell you a little more. But not here."

"You name the place," said Steve.

She thought for a moment, then said, "I have to sort out the boys here first, then I've got some business to attend to in the Campo Santa Maria Nova. Find the Miracoli church and ask your way to the second-hand bookshop. Give me an hour and I'll be in the back room. If you're there early, just browse – there's some interesting stuff."

"I'll check on its Hanseatic League section," he answered. Janice gave him a puzzled look before leaving him to see to her staff.

A few minutes later, having located the Miracoli church on his map, Steve left the café. He was very pleased with the way the morning was unfolding, and without any great effort on his part. He spent the next forty minutes strolling down the Strada Nova, then found the Miracoli church and had a cappuccino in the outside seating area in the square across the narrow canal from the church. He chose a seat which gave him a good view of the bookshop entrance. It was also a position where he could admire the skill of the gondoliers as they steered their craft past each other; in the narrowest part they were using their feet against the church wall.

Just before their agreed meeting time, Janice appeared around the corner of a *farmacia,* crossed the square and entered the bookshop. Steve followed her.

"Alex suggested we use his office at the back here," said Janice from behind a large stack of nineteenth century posters. As they moved into the office Alex pushed himself up from his computer chair. "I know when I'm not wanted," he said, giving Janice a friendly tap on the shoulder as she took his place and an exaggerated wink at Steve.

Steve perched himself on top of some small wooden library steps. "About Sergio," he began.

"There's a little bit of background first," said Janice. "My husband and I don't live in Venice, far too expensive. Also my great passion ever since I was a girl in England is riding. To buy a house and also have a paddock for a horse meant we had to live over the causeway in the Veneto."

Suddenly Steve could see where this was leading. "So where do you live?"

"On the edge of a small town called Marano."

"And how does that link up with Sergio?" he asked.

"Well one of the houses near ours is owned by Signora Foscolo, and she has a widowed daughter called Claudia.

Claudia, I don't know her married name, is a very smart-looking woman who works in Venice." She stopped for a moment as if unsure of herself. "You know, I really don't know much about her at all."

Steve, anxious for her to get to the point of her tale, curbed his impatience and gave what he hoped was an encouraging but non-committal, "Mm. But Sergio?"

"Oh yes, about a year ago," continued Janice, "or a bit more, perhaps a year and a half, I was out riding towards Scaltenego, although the name of the place doesn't matter, when I saw Claudia and Sergio. They were walking into a small ristorante on the edge of the town. I was a field away but I'm sure it was them. They're both quite striking looking."

"Was that the only time you saw them?" asked Steve.

"Oh no. Over the next couple of months I saw them together several times in and around the area. In fact I said to my husband that I thought something could be developing between those two. But like most men he wasn't interested."

"But it didn't develop," put in Steve.

"Obviously not, as far as I'm aware. There's been no sign of Sergio in our area for at least six months. And I've seen them pass in the street here in Venice and there's not been the flicker of a sign."

"Well it's something to think about. Thanks for letting me know," said Steve.

Janice got up, ready to leave. "If it helps in your search for Pinot," she said.

"Who knows?" he answered. "At the moment, the more I can find out about people who know him, the more chance I have of catching up with him in the short time I have left here."

He made his way out of the shop, leaving Janice talking to Alex, who had returned to reclaim his chair.

CHAPTER 16

After leaving Steve at the pasticceria, Macbride made his way back to his room. As he had spent most of the previous night playing the casino with Sergio, he felt more than justified in spending some time catching up on much needed sleep. As a result it was after eleven thirty before he was back in the San Polo area and was once more stepping from a wilderness masquerading as a front garden into the elegant mini-Empire over which Mr Parsons was head.

The young female secretary met him in the foyer, recognised him, and immediately took him into Mr Parsons' office. "You've arrived at the right time to catch him," she said. "He's just got back from making arrangements for Mr Alsobri's funeral."

Rather than leaving him there, she stood rather awkwardly and Macbride had the distinct impression she was about to say more. However, at that moment a very agitated Parsons arrived.

"Thank you, Adele. If you'd bring some coffee through?" said Parsons. The secretary left them and Parsons settled himself behind his desk.

"Please take a seat, Mr Macbride," he said. "I'm sorry if I appeared abrupt just now, but you would never believe the amount of red tape I have had to deal with regarding the funeral arrangements for Mr Alsobri."

Macbride had no interest in hearing about the funeral arrangements for a person he had never met, nor did he have any sympathy for the difficulties that Parsons, a man he had met only once, was encountering. However, while they were waiting for the coffee to arrive, he was prepared to listen with half an ear while Parsons aired his grievances about the multiple failings of the Italian administrative system.

"I was informed by head office that cremation was what they believed Mr Alsobri would have wanted, so that will take place, but only after I spent a good two hours of my time convincing a clerk that Charles' papers of residence were in order. Then almost all the rest of this morning has been taken up obtaining a place in the cemetery on the Isola San Michele in the lagoon here where his ashes can be held." He picked up a pen, twiddled it round and then looked at it as if he was wondering what it was, then put it back on his desk before adding, "And that included getting a letter signed by the priest in charge of the church here that verified that Charles was a practising Catholic."

"But you've managed it," said Macbride, just as Adele returned, as if on cue, to place two mugs and a cafetière of coffee on a small table. She smiled at him, and he realised she'd thought his remark was meant for her.

Parsons hardly noticed Adele or the coffee. His mind was still seething with annoyance at having been saddled with a responsibility that he was finding to be, at the very least, irksome. Adele, without being asked, poured the coffee then made to leave them.

Macbride felt he could wait no longer. "Did the notebook turn up?" he asked. "Or did that magazine chap get in touch with you?"

Adele quietly closed the door, and Parsons shook his head. Although Macbride was disappointed, Parsons' next response showed that he was more concerned with his own problems than with any queries Macbride might wish to put to him. Macbride felt himself to be a complete irrelevance in the man's present state of mind. He began to dislike him, wrapped up as he was in his own affairs.

"The only thing I can thank them for," began Parsons, "the only thing, and it's only minor, is that they gave me a location plan of the cemetery and marked on it the place where the ashes will be placed. They said that, any time in the future, it would save me, or anyone else for that matter, having to queue at the office to get the information."

"Well that's always something you've achieved," said Macbride, making little attempt to hide his sarcasm.

Parsons nodded his agreement. He seemed to notice his coffee for the first time and took a careful sip. "Yes," he said, "I mustn't lose this or I'll probably have to go through the whole rigmarole again."

He pulled a wallet out of his inside jacket pocket, took from it an A5 piece of paper and spread it out on the table. Macbride leant forward and saw it was headed 'Cimitero' and that it was a plan of the layout of the cemetery with the times when it was open to the public. A line had been drawn, in yellow felt pen, from the cemetery entrance to the bottom corner of the plan. To indicate some interest, he followed the line with his finger.

"It's a very big place," said Parsons, "so rather than be wandering round like a lost soul – no pun intended there! – they marked that on for me." He gave a hesitant smile.

"Useful," was all Macbride could think to say.

"True," agreed Parsons, "but once you're in the general area you need to have the information on the back of the sheet." He turned the sheet over and pointed. "*Recinto, Fila, Verticale,*" he read out. "That's the enclosure, the row, and the level. And you simply use the numbers written there to find the right spot."

Macbride was now intensely interested. He could hardly believe his eyes. The numbers he was now looking at were three sets of two figures; not the same as those on Pinot's card, but sufficiently similar for him to feel this was a lead that couldn't be ignored. He checked his watch; Steve would have already met Rosario and his cousin, so the Adelaide at six would be their next rendezvous. He hoped, but doubted, that Steve would be having the same luck that hard work brings.

"Can I treat you to lunch, Mr Parsons?" he asked expansively, as he was now viewing the man in the most kindly of lights.

"Well that would be extremely kind of you," Parsons said. "I rarely have the pleasure, but there is a nearby trattoria which is highly regarded. If you'll just give me a few minutes to inform the staff of my whereabouts and to get my outdoor coat."

Almost as soon as he had left the office, Adele returned. She had come ostensibly to take away the coffee things, but she spoke to Macbride in a hurried whisper with several anxious glances back towards the door.

"I don't know why Mr Parsons says he doesn't know the military man, because he does," she said. "The two of them have met many times during the year I've been here."

"To do with the business here?" asked a puzzled Macbride.

"No. I just assumed it was something to do with Lega Nord, as I think Mr Parsons is a big supporter."

They heard Parsons returning and Adele picked up the tray.

"That coffee was superb," said Macbride. "Thank you."

"Adele has all the qualities one could ask for in a personal assistant," said Parsons as he appeared in the doorway ready to go for his promised lunch. Macbride smiled at Adele and nodded his appreciation to her.

"Perhaps you could make a start on those monthly returns in my absence," said Parsons. Clearly he was very conscious of maintaining his image of business-like efficiency, but if Adele was to be believed, he had other interests than trade links.

Although the lunch was excellent, Macbride found the conversation frustratingly irrelevant. He needed time to consider the implications of Adele's revelation, to inform

Steve, and perhaps also to seek Agnew's view about the company Parsons and Alsobri had been keeping.

* * *

Steve, now confident in his knowledge of the vaporetto routes, took the number one boat down to the Arsenale stop. From there he walked along the Riva di Ca di Dio, went over a small bridge onto the Riva San Biagio, then turned left away from the lagoon into the Via Garibaldi. It was well before the ten-thirty meeting time Rosario had suggested; there was time for him to loiter.

Looking up the broad street, he was struck by the lack of ornate, expensive buildings. There were a number of small shops selling everyday items and a few bars and trattorias, but none of them with boards outside displaying menus to tempt tourists. This was an area which was almost set apart from the rest of the city, as here tourism did not reign. Although vastly different from the Cannareggio canal area, for Steve it had the same feeling of being the sort of area where ordinary people lived and worked.

However, an inscribed plaque on the first house he came to informed him that this had not always been so; the area had historical connections. John and Sebastian Cabot, the Venetian navigators, had lived there and in 1497 they had discovered Newfoundland. Steve made a mental note to see if Macbride was aware of that, although knowing Macbride, he was sure he would be. As he wandered on he realised he wouldn't have time for a proper lunch.

Further up the street there was a food stall where he bought a *porchetta panino* and a bottle of water and ate and drank as he strolled. As he approached the point where the street split into two, on the right-hand side he came to the gates leading into the public gardens and, as if placed to guard them, the large bronze statue of Garibaldi. Steve leaned on the metal railings and, like any good tourist, had a good look at it. He watched the terrapins in the pool surrounding the statue; some were sunning themselves on rocks, while others were making valiant but vain efforts to climb the vertical concrete surrounding walls.

There were still five minutes to the half hour, so he moved round and was looking at the statue of a soldier, which was back to back with Garibaldi, when he became aware of a man sitting on a park bench apparently absorbed in reading a newspaper. As soon as he saw Steve looking his way he folded his paper and stood up. It was Rosario.

Steve casually walked across to a waste bin and threw his empty water bottle in, then followed Rosario, who had gone further into the park. There were few people around; he saw a couple of joggers and a young woman pushing a baby in a pushchair. Steve was surprised by the large area of cut grass, the number of trees and shrubs and some well-tended flower beds. It struck him as being a haven of tranquillity, which was shattered when a group of young lads ran past him and began kicking a football around. But his attention was mainly concerned with where Rosario was leading him; he had taken a diagonal path towards what appeared to be a three-storey block of flats.

Steve had kept about thirty yards back, but he increased his pace when Rosario turned a corner of the block. However, he need not have worried, as Rosario was waiting there for him.

"It's flat 7," he said, "on the ground floor. Beppe knows you're coming and why. I'll stay out here to enjoy the fresh air and read my paper and to check that you haven't been followed."

Steve halted. "What do you mean, followed?"

"Yesterday, after we'd spoken, when I was on my way to lunch, I was stopped by two men who asked me about you. I told them you'd admired my drawings but I knew nothing about you. They said they were police, but I know they weren't and I checked with a friend at the Parlamento bar…"

"Gianni," broke in Steve.

"Yes, Gianni. We are both born and bred Venetians. The city of Venice is only a city to visitors; to us, it is a village. Between us we know all the locals. These other men are not locals and Gianni knows they are dangerous and he told me to take care."

"Thanks, Rosario," said Steve. Then just as he was about to go into the block a thought struck him. "Will there be a language problem with Beppe?" he asked. He had fully expected Rosario to be with them.

Rosario smiled. "He's worked on English cruise ships for more than twenty years. He might even speak it better than an Irishman."

There was no time for a riposte from Steve as Rosario turned and strode away. The entrance door had been left open slightly, held there by a small piece of metal cast in the shape of an anchor. Steve pushed his way in, found the door of Number 7 and knocked. It was opened almost immediately by a small, dapper man casually dressed in jeans and a T-shirt.

"Not captain's table garb I'm afraid, but Rosi's message only reached me half an hour ago," he said, indicating his clothing and giving Steve a welcoming smile and a handshake. That one sentence convinced Steve that Rosario's comment about Beppe's language skills was spot on.

"I'm very grateful you could see me at such short notice," he replied.

Beppe waved a hand which simultaneously dismissed the remark and indicated the armchair for him to take. "I took the liberty of pouring a glass of wine for each of us when I saw you approaching," he said. He placed the glass on a small table beside the chair.

"I don't know if Rosario told you," continued Steve, settling himself, "but Pinot and I are old friends from way back and as I've unexpectedly found myself in Venice for a few days I thought I'd look him up. Unfortunately I don't have his address with me."

"Mm," said Beppe sorrowfully. "Rosario didn't tell me that. He just said you wanted to know about the boat trips Pinot and I have made." He leaned back in his chair and spread his hands.

Steve shrugged. "That's a pity. But if you tell me about your trips it might gave me a clue as to where I can enquire further. I've got two more days and Pinot would be far from pleased if he found out I hadn't made every effort to find him."

"Well to start with, the boat is mine. Fourteen feet, old but very sound with an excellent sixteen horsepower outboard. Could manage with a smaller one, but if you're well out, say Torcello way, and the weather turns, it's good to have the extra power to get back home quicker."

"When Pinot went with you, was it for fishing or just enjoying the lagoon and the islands?" asked Steve, keen to find out more than just the capabilities of the boat.

"Some fishing trips, yes. Some visits to islands. Pinot has a great liking for the Armenian island. He can talk to the monks there in their own tongue. He's a very well-educated man – but you probably know that."

Steve, not wanting to stop Beppe's flow, again simply nodded.

"Certosa was another one," the Italian went on. "That was when it was just being developed with a hotel and a brand new vaporetto stop. Pinot had a bit of a bee in his bonnet about the fragility of the lagoon's ecosystem. He reckoned it was close to tipping point."

"And is it?"

Beppe didn't answer immediately, then, with a rueful smile he said, "That really depends on who you ask."

"What about any other places you landed on?" asked Steve.

"Well last time we were out, about three or four days ago, Pinot said he had to relieve himself." Steve did a rapid mental calculation; that would be the day, or perhaps two days, before he and Macbride had forced their way into Pinot's warehouse. "We landed on cemetery island. It was after normal opening hours, so I moored up beside where they're doing the extension to the island and stayed with the boat while Pinot scrambled ashore. The authorities wouldn't have been best pleased if they'd found us there. I wasn't very happy about it, especially when he took longer than he said he would. But we got away with it."

"And the pair of you won't be going back," said Steve.

"Correct," answered Beppe. "Or definitely not in my boat. But we get on well and Pinot's a good boat companion, so we'll be out together again, perhaps even to check out some of the tiny uninhabited islands like we did last autumn."

"What was special about them?"

"Pinot is never happy unless he has a cause to support," said Beppe. "I think another friend of his had hinted that there was something going on there."

"A friend who might help me locate Pinot?" asked Steve, trying hard not to appear too anxious for the information.

"A man who seems to have some sort of watching brief over the lagoon and all the islands, especially the small uninhabited ones."

"Did Pinot mention his name?"

At that moment the door of Beppe's apartment was suddenly thrown open and two men entered. "Beppe, your boat's adrift in the Rio di San Giuseppe and it's causing some problems," said one of them.

"Right I'm coming," Beppe answered immediately, pushing himself out of his chair. "I'll see you again when this is sorted," he said to Steve as he made for the door.

Steve nodded and followed him out. The two men were hurrying away down the corridor. Steve wondered how much they'd heard of the conversation between him and Beppe. He found it hard to believe that a man as experienced as Beppe would have left his boat in a state where it would have caused problems for others.

After leaving the block, Steve saw no sign of Rosario. He made his way to the edge of the public gardens. Turning right, he started to walk briskly along the *fondamenta* bordering the lagoon. He kept up this brisk pace until he was in the Riva Degli Schiavoni and reached the equestrian statue of Vittorio Emanuele II. He paused to admire it and at the same time check the way he had come. A beer at the nearest outdoor seating area gave him the same opportunity before he paid, moved quickly across the next bridge and boarded the incoming number one vaporetto at the San Zaccaria Danieli stop. He left it at San Marcuola and walked the rest of the way to his apartment.

On the journey back he reflected on his day's work. Reluctantly he came to the conclusion that there were only two points that Macbride might consider relevant; first, that Sergio had for a time had contact with Claudia, and second, that Rosario was of the same opinion as Gianni about other 'dangerous' men being interested in their activities in Venice. Unfortunately, much as he had liked Beppe, he felt the information he had given him would not be considered progress by Macbride when he met up with him at the Adelaide that evening.

CHAPTER 17

Steve wasn't looking forward to the evening meeting; he felt he hadn't achieved a great deal, and time was running away from them. However, when he arrived at the bar Macbride was already there, seated at a table for two at the far end of the long ground floor room. He appeared to be in a remarkably upbeat mood.

"What progress, Steve?" The question was asked before Steve had actually sat down.

"A mixed bag, really. Interesting chat with Janice, but my meeting with Rosario's cousin, Beppe, was abruptly terminated by a couple of blokes who didn't seem to want him talking to me."

"More of Gianni's 'persone indesiderabili'?" suggested Macbride.

"Struck me that way."

"Well, let's get ourselves organised with the food here and then we can swap notes."

"OK," said Steve, glancing round for a menu board, "if you know what's on offer."

"I've already had a chat with Marco, he and his wife own the place, and he reckons the plates of mixed fish, fresh in this afternoon, are very good and very good value."

Marco, who was already approaching their table, overheard and added, "And that includes the *moeche*, soft-shelled crabs, which are at their very best just now. And cooked in egg and parmesan batter they are better than superb."

"I'll go along with that," said Steve.

Macbride nodded his agreement to Marco. "So that will be two, and with it a decent bottle of white."

"We have a very good bottle from the Dolomites, just perfect for this meal."

When Marco had gone to inform the chef of their order, Macbride leaned forward. "OK, Steve, let's have the blow-by-blow account of your day's work."

Steve began with the first of his conversations with Janice, when she'd told him about the visit of the bogus finance officers.

"It looks as though they, whoever they are, are pulling out all the stops to get ahead of us," was Macbride's only comment. However, he was much more interested when he heard about the meetings between Sergio and Claudia. "I wonder why it started, why it ended, and who ended it," he mused.

"I can certainly think of several reasons why it might have started," said Steve. "She certainly ticks all the right boxes."

Macbride chose to ignore the comment, but his frown of concentration suggested to Steve that he was not thinking of her physical attractions but of the possible outcomes of their meetings. Then, putting that to one side, he said, "And what about your meeting with the cousin of Rosario?"

"Very pleasant chap, easy to get on with," answered Steve. "I got the distinct impression that he and Pinot had a lot in common. But he didn't have an address for him, didn't even know of his art store house. In fact, after he'd finished extolling the virtues of his boat, all he told me was about their trips out on the lagoon."

"But did he name any other people, or mention any particular places they went to?"

"No individuals," answered Steve. "Over the last year they made quite a few trips to an island where a group of Armenian monks live. Beppe said it was because Pinot liked to talk to them in their own language. Other than that they were mainly all fishing trips, except once at the back end of last year when they went to an island called Certosa where a hotel was being built and a new vaporetto stop was being made for it, so they both went ashore to check it out. And on an evening trip last week they stopped at another place for Pinot to go ashore – he needed to relieve himself."

"And where was that?" asked Macbride, without any great interest, as he was beginning to feel that Steve was right in his assessment of the value of the information Beppe had given. But Steve's answer had him sitting bolt upright, intensely interested.

"It was San Michele, the cemetery island," said Steve.

Just at that moment Marco brought the bottle of wine, opened it and glanced at Macbride and then at each of the two empty glasses in turn. "It'll be fine Marco, just leave it, we'll pour it," said Macbride. Marco went off to see to his other customers.

Macbride rubbed his hands together and smiled at Steve. "Between us we seem to have found two pieces of the jigsaw."

"Go on," said Steve.

Macbride told him of the plan of the cemetery which Parsons had shown him and the system which was used to identify the location of every individual's remains. "And you reckon the three sets of figures on the back of one of Pinot's cards fit into that system?" said Steve.

"I'd stake your pension on it," said Macbride. "Except that to be a perfect fit it needs a slight alteration. I'll explain in a moment, but here's our food." Two plates bearing more than ample portions were placed in front of them by Marco. "Buon appetito," he said.

They began eating but Steve quickly put his fork down. "Good though this is, I think I'll enjoy it more when you have put me right in the picture."

"OK, but I'll talk and eat at the same time. As it happens I ended up with two very interesting pieces of information, but I'll start with the cemetery plan. The numbers I wrote down from Pinot's card don't fit into the plan exactly. At least the top two don't. But I was convinced there was a link, so after Parsons and I had lunch and he went back to his office, I went back to my homely abode and looked more closely at the figures I had. I don't suppose you remember them?"

"Not exactly," answered Steve.

"Well, I had written down eight eight, zero six, three

two. On Parson's plan there was no eight eight, but I noticed an area labelled eight B. As all the figures on the card had been pencilled in and were very faint I reckon I'd mistaken the second letter B for an 8."

"So the location that Pinot wanted to lead us to is 8B, 06, 32," said Steve.

"That's it and it's on San Michele, the island Pinot landed on just last week after the normal closing time for visitors," said Macbride.

"So, I presume that's where we'll be headed when we've done full justice to this?" Steve started tucking into his meal once more.

"The opening hours this time of year are seven-thirty in the morning to six o'clock in the evening. No need for us to rush away from here. We'll check it out in the morning."

"Sounds as though it might be a very revealing trip," said Steve. "But you also said you had another piece of information."

"That's right. A real surprise, and at the moment I can't see how it fits in. It seems Sergio and Parsons knew each other, had done for a couple of years at least."

"Yesterday Parsons told you he didn't even know Sergio's name?"

Macbride brushed the interruption aside. "Parsons' secretary, Adele, managed to have a few words with me when Parsons was out of the room. She struck me as being as honest as the day is long and she informed me that Parsons and the military man definitely knew each other and they'd met several times in his office."

Steve pursed his lips. "They knew each other and they

met," he repeated. "Why?"

"Adele said she thought it might be Lega Nord business, but she wasn't sure. Whatever the reason, I'm going to have to inform Agnew and then pay Mr Parsons another call."

"After our cemetery visit?"

"Probably Monday when he'll be back at work and Agnew will have had time to make enquiries and may have some information for me. Now our arrangements for the morning." He pulled out a map of the vaporetto routes. "The number 52 boat calls in at Cimitero on its way to Murano; you can pick it up at the Tre Archi stop. I'll get the first boat leaving Guglie after eight, but sometimes on Sundays the early boats are taken off, so I'll stand on the outside deck. Look out for me; if I'm there, board at Tre Archi. And don't forget to dress accordingly, it's a cemetery we'll be going to, not a bordello." He flashed a grin at no one in particular before adding, "But there's no need for us to be po-faced tonight."

He put up his hand and attracted the attention of Francesca, Marco's partner. "That was superb, just as Marco had promised," he said, passing a hand over his empty plate and the bottle of wine.

Francesca smiled. "Thank you. Would you like to see the dessert menu?"

Macbride looked across at Steve, who was in the process of using a piece of bread to ensure he cleaned his plate thoroughly. "I assume your *torta della casa* will not let you down, so I'll go for that and I'll have a *sgroppino* to follow."

"I'm sure you won't be disappointed," said Francesca, and then she turned to Steve with a questioning look.

"Yes, make that two," said Steve.

The *torta di ricotta e uvetta* certainly didn't disappoint, and the *sgroppino* had just the right amount of vodka to give it the distinctive kick.

"An *espresso doppio* will finish things off nicely," said Macbride to Marco.

"Again, make that two," put in Steve.

"And by the way, Marco," Macbride added, "do you know Sergio, the ex-Air Force man? Tall, always smartly dressed?"

"Yes, I know him, but he only comes in here now and again. Not regular. Francesca went to school with his daughter." Francesca came across to the table when she heard her name. "I'm talking about Sergio's daughter, Maria," said Marco.

"Oh yes. There were four of us who were big friends until we left school. Three of us are still very close, but Maria went to university in Parma to do a medical degree and after that I think she went abroad to do voluntary work. She didn't keep in touch with any of the rest of the group and I suppose she was too far away to come to our annual school reunions."

"That happens in a lot of cases, good intentions and all that," said Steve.

"I knew her father," said Macbride, "on business matters, but I never met Maria or her mother."

"Her mother died when Maria was about fourteen or fifteen," Marco went on. "It was a real tragedy; a plane crash in the Adriatic and hers was one of the bodies that was never found. Maria took it badly and I imagine her father did as well. The two of them became very close."

“But a few years later she went away to university,” said Steve.

“I think it was really a make or break, if you know what I mean,” said Marco.

Both Macbride and Steve nodded their understanding. Then, as the conversation seemed to have come to a natural end, Marco said, ”I’ll bring your coffees now,” and he and Francesca moved away.

They took their time over the coffee.

“I could get to like this lifestyle,” said Steve.

“Who wouldn’t,” agreed Macbride. “The only thing that’s spoiling it for me is the company I’m having to keep.”

“I assume you mean in your rooming place,” said Steve.

They both smiled, then left the restaurant and went their separate ways.

CHAPTER 18

It was seven-thirty when Steve left his apartment, too early for the vaporetto, so he made his way to the Parlamento. The staff were carrying out tables and chairs and arranging them along the twenty yards of canalside that fronted the bar. He took an outside seat and almost immediately he was joined by Gloria, who stood in front of him in an attitude that suggested she was not happy with his presence.

"I don't think Gianni will want to talk to you," she began, but Steve held up his hand to interrupt her.

"All I want is a coffee, but I was going to ask how he is."

"He's back at work today and he says he's OK, but I don't think he's really got over it yet."

"It was a nasty, unnerving experience for him," said Steve. "Very frightening."

"I'll bring your coffee now," she replied, obviously not at

all keen to have an extended conversation. She came back with the coffee and he paid her. As she turned to go he said, "I'm leaving in a few days, so tell him thanks."

She gave a thin smile. "I will."

As he drank the coffee he thought of taking the number 52 vaporetto from Guglie, but that wasn't the arrangement and wouldn't have pleased Macbride. Besides, the walk back to the Tre Archi bridge and then over it and along to the Tre Archi stop would give him the chance to see if anyone was attempting to trail him.

There was no trail, but as the vaporetto drew in he saw a soberly-dressed man standing on the outside passenger deck: Macbride. Steve boarded, made his way past Macbride and a few others, and stood on the further side of the boat. No sign of recognition passed between Steve and Macbride.

The boat made its way out of the canal into the waters of the lagoon where there was a distinct swell, along with waves caused by passing craft. To Steve it seemed a rather boring and lengthy journey between the next three stops. The only interesting feature was an open concreted area, at the entrance to a minor canal leading into the city, with two fuel pumps. Three water taxis were waiting their turn to be filled up ready for their day's work. The thought struck him that security could be tighter around such a possible explosive fire risk. He stored the idea as the boat turned away from the city to head the short distance across the lagoon to Isola di San Michele, the cemetery island. It was a beautiful morning now. The sun was warm, the sky a duck-egg blue, and in the far distance to the north, the Dolomite mountains could be clearly seen, their highest peaks still snow-capped.

As the boat began to edge its way into the San Michele stop, Steve moved across and stood beside Macbride. "Any particular plans when we disembark?" he asked in little more than a whisper.

Macbride nodded. "When we get there, you go into the office on the left and pick up a couple of maps of the place. I'll go to the shop and buy some flowers. It's the done thing," he added, in answer to Steve's unspoken question.

When the boat was tied up there was a sudden rush of about a dozen passengers, all heading to the flower shop.

"Looks as though they've got other plans for the day and want to get this over with quickly," observed Steve.

"You could be right," answered Macbride. "I might be stuck in a queue. You can do the tourist bit, have a look around, and we'll meet up in area 8B in half an hour."

Steve had no queue to contend with, and as there were several piles of maps on a table just inside the office, within minutes he was strolling past the flower shop and into the main entrance.

The first thing that struck him was the general air of calm that pervaded the place. There were sweeping areas of lawns and mature trees, and the soft sound of birdsong. The path he was on led towards the church, but he decided to explore parts of the actual cemetery area. Using the map he picked out the Evangelista area, where the graves of some celebrated English people and Americans were located. As it was also fairly near 8B, that settled it for him.

When he reached the area, he was disturbed to see that although the surrounds of the famous were well tended, much of the rest was overgrown. Perversely he made his way to the unkempt area and tried to make out the inscriptions on several of the gravestones. Many of them had been badly eroded by the weather and defeated his efforts to decipher them. However, he felt a sudden pang for a lad named only 'Jack' from Tunbridge Wells, who had drowned in a shipwreck in the lagoon in the 1800s. In contrast to that, he was amused by a stone which stated that another of the long departed 'has Left us in Peace'.

Making his way into the well-tended area, he noted that there were no visitors yet gathered around the graves of the famous, presumably because it was too early in the morning for the tourists. He doubted if Macbride would ask him about Brodsky, Clarke or Pound, so he retraced his steps towards the church and found the brick steps leading to the 8B area. Here there were no graves with headstones, just block-paved aisles with row upon row of marble-faced drawers resembling huge filing cabinets. Most of them had names and dates inscribed on them and some also had photographs of the deceased. But the topmost rows had neither, and were obviously waiting their turn to be brought into use.

Macbride was already in the 06 aisle when Steve turned into it. He saw him at the far end pushing the metal platform ladder which was there to enable visitors to reach the higher levels of drawers. Number 32 was close to where Steve was standing, but it was at the second highest level, so he waited for Macbride and the ladder to arrive.

"You just stand there Steve, this is man's work," said Macbride sarcastically as he carefully positioned the ladder.

"An appropriate choice of flowers," answered Steve, nodding towards the small bunch of plastic red roses which Macbride was picking up from the platform.

"It's worth remembering that the human touch in a place like this never goes amiss," retorted Macbride. "And I believe Pinot was proud of his father's Lancastrian roots."

That was news to Steve, and in any case he had not been referring to the roses and their colour but the fact that the flowers were plastic and as a result presumably cheap.

"Hang on to them while I check 32, then we'll donate them somewhere," said Macbride as he climbed up to the second topmost level. He checked both directions to make sure there was no one else in their aisle, then quietly called out "Bingo!" to Steve. He had taken out from behind the drawer handle a small package wrapped in polythene.

He rapidly descended the ladder and together he and Steve pushed it several yards along the aisle. "Ditch those flowers," said Macbride. "We'll examine our package away from this area."

Steve laid the plastic flowers at the base of the next aisle round the corner, and they made their way back towards the church. Near it there was an empty bench seat, and it was there that Macbride unwrapped the package and spread out the single page it contained.

"Obviously he was in a hurry," observed Steve, glancing at the two lines of scrawled writing. Silently the two of them read: 'Not island drone for Ionian Pride. 7/04 Fenice Maria Stuarda 7/04'.

On the vaporetto heading back to the city, they both agreed they would need help making some sense of the message. "I'll make enquiries," said Macbride, "perhaps with Parsons, perhaps with Sergio, but that's debatable in both cases, and Agnew might have some thoughts. And, of course, you've got a date with Claudia tomorrow morning; she might have some idea."

"There's a lot of hope involved here," said Steve in a rather downcast fashion.

"Buck up, Steve. Remember Pound never gave up hope, even when he was imprisoned in that outside cage near Pisa."

"Pound?" queried Steve.

"Ezra Pound. Surely you visited his grave. Has none of my culture rubbed off on you?"

Steve gritted his teeth and made no reply.

They travelled back to the main island on the same vaporetto, but not together. It was only after they had both got off at the Guglie stop that Macbride spoke. He had obviously been mulling over the situation, as there was no preamble.

"As it's Sunday we can't contact Sergio, even if we decided we wanted to, or Parsons, but I'll definitely see him tomorrow when you're seeing Claudia. So that just leaves Agnew. I'll contact him and see if he can come up with something."

"In the meantime, what about lunch at Andrea's place?"

"Yeah," agreed Macbride. "It'll also give us time to think as well as me contacting Agnew. Let's say two o'clock."

* * *

Steve arrived at the restaurant a few minutes before Macbride, but when he saw him striding along from the Guglie bridge, he waited for him and introduced him to Andrea. The sky had become overcast, and Andrea suggested they should take an indoor table.

"Might just be the turn of the tide," said Macbride.

Andrea shook his head. "I don't think it will rain, but it will be quite cool beside the canal."

"Local knowledge," said Steve as they followed Andrea.

When they were seated, Steve was happy to go along with Andrea's choice, but not Macbride. Having been told that *carciofi* were artichokes, he explained "artichokes and I don't get on." Eventually he settled on cutlet of lamb with potatoes.

"It might take about a quarter of an hour," said Andrea.

"That's no problem," said Macbride. "Just send a couple of beers across to help pass the time."

When the beers arrived, Macbride picked up his glass and held it up towards Steve in an approving fashion, then took a long, satisfying swig. "Now that's a good honest beer," he pronounced.

Steve took a careful, considered drink and agreed. "Almost as good as an Anarchy beer brewed near Newcastle."

"You'll have to introduce me to it when we return if it's that good."

Any further drinking and commenting on the respective merits of beers was suddenly interrupted by Andrea arriving with a distressed-looking Rosario close behind him. "Gianni from the Parlamento told him you might be here," Andrea explained before he left them.

"Pull up a chair," said Steve to Rosario before he introduced him to Macbride. "This is Rosario, the artist friend of Pinot and Beppe's cousin."

The two men simply nodded to each other.

"What brings you here?" asked Steve.

"It's about Beppe," Rosario began.

"He left me very suddenly yesterday," said Steve. "Something about his boat being adrift and causing a problem in a narrow channel."

Rosario shook his head. "I've just come from the hospital. He's in a bad way, but they say he'll survive."

"Why? What happened?"

"Evidently when Beppe got to the jetty the two men who'd told him about the boat were there already. But the boat was exactly as he'd left it; properly moored. It had just been a ploy to get him there alone. That particular mooring is well concealed by a line of shrubs. They started beating him up with metal bars. They would probably have killed him if a group of cadets from the naval school hadn't been passing that way and heard his shouts for help. They weighed in and the attackers ran off."

"Did they have any idea who these men were?" asked Steve.

"No. The lads didn't recognise them and in any case their main concern was to get medical help for Beppe. They called for the ambulance launch and it was there within minutes, they said."

"I'm pleased they did," said Steve.

"Beppe was very anxious that you should know. That's why I'm here, but I am very concerned. These men are dangerous and I don't know if Beppe or I can help you any more."

Macbride, who had been listening carefully but had said nothing so far, answered him. "What the pair of you have done is valuable to Steve in his search for Pinot, but there's no way we want to put you in any further danger. Thanks for informing us, and please also thank Beppe."

Rosario nodded. "We only want Pinot to be safe. He is a good man, a good friend." With that he quickly made his way out of the restaurant.

Steve and Macbride drank their beer in silence, each with his own thoughts, until Andrea arrived with their food and a bottle of Bardolino.

"I took the liberty of adding this," he said, as he placed it on the table with two glasses.

"Much appreciated, but don't spoil us too much," said Macbride with a smile. "We might get used to it."

Andrea left them and they talked as they ate, first about the food, which was excellent, then about yesterday's attack on Beppe. Macbride was silent for a while as he drank the wine. Finally he summed up his thoughts.

"I reckon they still think we don't know what message Pinot is trying to get out."

"Well in a way they're right, aren't they?" stated Steve bluntly.

Macbride nodded. "If they thought we did know they'd be attacking us, not Gianni or Beppe."

"So finding the message is still very important," said Steve.

"No," answered Macbride. "We've found it, we're just not sure what it means. Unfortunately, like fools, instead of taking the card with the numbers written on the back we just made a note of the numbers, and the card is still in his art store place. If they find the card and do as we did and find there is no message, they'll be after us."

"So when do we revisit his bolt hole to get the card?"

"I haven't got the key to the padlock on me," said

Macbride. "In any case it would be better to use the side door, if you've got your picks."

"Never travel without them," answered Steve. "If we take our time over the wine and then coffee it'll be late afternoon when we get down there."

* * *

It was just after five when they reached the corner where Janice's bar stood. There were still a good number of people in the main thoroughfare, most of them heading for the station. However, the cool breeze and the overcast sky made them more concerned with reaching their destination than dawdling en route.

Macbride and Steve turned into the side street. There were no customers sitting at the outside tables of the trattoria further along from the alley leading to Pinot's side door. They quickly reached it, Steve with his picks ready.

They were not needed. The door had been smashed in around the lock and the lower panel. It stood half open. Not much finesse used here, thought Steve.

Macbride indicated that they should move a few yards back up the alley to consider the situation. "I'm stating the obvious," he began, "but whoever tried to force their way in there, breaking the lock wasn't enough. There was also a bolt to contend with."

Steve nodded. "Which means someone was already in there, and that someone could well be Pinot."

"And we might be too late," added Macbride grimly.

They moved back to the door and he slowly pushed it wide enough for them to enter, though he was unable to prevent it making a scraping noise on the stone floor. Cautiously they moved in and crouched down, listening. Two minutes passed and there was only silence. A further minute passed, and then they heard a faint shuffling noise coming from the ground floor which could have been someone moving to ease a cramped limb.

Macbride tapped Steve on the shoulder and indicated that he should make his way up to the mezzanine while he would take the ground floor. Steve took out his pencil torch, but did not switch it on. Moving extremely slowly and still in a crouched position, he inched his way to the foot of the stairs. Using his left hand for balance, he climbed two stairs, then waited, listening. Silence.

Two more stairs and this time he became aware of the sound of breathing coming from somewhere below him. Macbride, who had reached the foot of the stairs, also heard it. Steve stayed where he was but stretched his hand holding the torch to the level of the top step, switched it on and directed the thin beam down into the ground floor area.

Then two things happened simultaneously; a shot rang out, the bullet narrowly missing Steve's torch hand before smacking into the wall behind him, and Macbride launched himself at the gunman, bringing him crashing to the ground. The gun clattered onto the floor beyond the reach of either of them.

Macbride's charge had carried him beyond the gunman, who scrambled to his feet and raced to the door. As he made his escape from the warehouse, Macbride was still extricating himself from the remains of a smashed desk and clambering to his feet.

Steve, who had moved to the mezzanine landing, had his torch beam on Macbride, and he now saw a second man come out from behind a large easel. In his right hand he had a large, curved blade. He raised it, ready to plunge into Macbride's unprotected back.

For Steve there was no time for considered, rational thought; training allied to instinct took over. One leap took him onto the top of the mezzanine banister railing and, almost in the same movement, he flung himself onto the head and shoulders of the man. Given Steve's training, the struggle for the knife could only have one victor.

Macbride got to his feet and looked at Steve admiringly. "Thanks for that. Still ready for action, then," he said. He looked down at the man's body, the eyes now staring in death. "Just a shame he won't be able to tell us anything."

"Yes, sorry about that," said Steve.

"Before we search this place, let me tell you that if our positions had been reversed I would have been up there. I would have calmly but quickly made my way down here to help you. And by then you would have been dead. Just as well I sent you up there."

"Don't mention it, I've got plenty to thank you for," replied Steve. "Now let's find the main light switch."

When the light came on they saw a scene of devastation; the contents of the place had been virtually destroyed. There was hardly a piece of furniture standing in its original position. Chairs had been overturned, one of the chair legs had been smashed off and the desk drawers and their contents had been scattered over the floor. The big display trolley was on its side with paintings strewn all over the floor.

“I’ll admit to the damage to the desk,” said Macbride, “but not the rest.”

The part of the room which had been Pinot’s work area, with several works in progress, had been dealt with in the same destructive way, and there were streaks of red paint on the wall. Macbride moved closer to the wall and shone his torch down the streaks. He stepped back and spoke to Steve, who had been sifting through the contents of the spilled drawers.

“This is not paint, Steve,” he said. “It’s blood, and that looks like part of a handprint to me.”

Steve gave it a cursory glance and nodded his agreement. They moved back to the stairs. Both of them had a good idea what they would find there.

They were right. Pinot’s body was on the bed; apart from trousers and socks, he was naked. His chest had been slashed in several places and his right hand had been severed. The mattress on which he was lying was soaked in blood. There was clearly nothing they could do for him.

“Poor bugger,” said Macbride. “Half an hour earlier and we might have prevented this.” Steve nodded grimly. “This time it’s for real for him,” he said, thinking back to the coffin at Mountsett crematorium.

Looking down at Pinot’s right arm, Macbride realised that there was no hand on the end of it. “Let’s get back down and check there again,” he said. Steve followed him back to the spot where they had seen the handprint on the wall. They found the severed hand lying behind the broken desk. The ends of each finger and the thumb down to the first joint had been cut off.

"So did they get him to talk, or not?" said Macbride. "And if he did, did he tell the truth?"

They turned their attention to the scattered contents of the drawers, and there among the debris Macbride found Pinot's cards.

"It looks as though they were overlooked, or not considered important," he said. He gathered them up and put them in his pocket.

Reasoning that there was nothing further to be gained from staying there any longer and not wanting to have to explain their presence to anyone who might turn up, they turned off the light and made their way out of the building. Macbride managed to pull the door shut and heard the lock click.

"I'll get word to Agnew about this," he said. "It'll be up to him to arrange for Pinot's disposal."

"I'll leave all that to you," Steve replied. "I'll just get back to my place and have a few beers. I need to try to make some sense out of what's happened, and what we know so far."

Macbride nodded. "And, with a bit of luck, tomorrow morning you'll get some information from Claudia. I'm going to have another chat with Parsons, but this time I intend to get the truth out of him. I'll ring you when I've finished with him."

Macbride strode off towards his rooming place while Steve, at a more leisurely pace, walked to the Tre Archi bridge. There was no boat on the canal, no men watching his apartment. He wondered if it was too early for them; or perhaps Pinot had been forced to give them the information they were after.

Back in his apartment, he opened a can of beer and tried to put himself into the mindset of Pinot's killers. If they had made him talk, did it matter? Probably not, if he hadn't got a message out. And as they'd missed the Queen of Spades card, it was more than likely that they were unaware of that pencilled message. If that was the case, he reckoned that if Claudia and Agnew had managed to make sense of it, then the odds on them getting the right result would have shortened considerably.

CHAPTER 19

At five minutes to ten Steve arrived at the Campo San Marcuola. As Claudia had said, there were two vaporetto stops, and today, thanks to her, he would be travelling in style rather than travelling with the tourists. With that thought in mind, he strolled along past the back of the church and sat on the edge of the raised level of the square facing a short wooden jetty. For the next few minutes he watched the crowds scurrying to and from the boats. Precisely at ten o'clock, a sleek, expensive-looking private launch nosed its way alongside the jetty.

"Morning Steve," called Claudia. "Pleased you could make it."

The driver was in the process of looping a rope around a pole of the jetty. He offered a helping hand to Steve, who ignored it and then, to soften what could have been taken for a snub, he said, "I'm happy with this sort of craft".

Claudia gave the driver's shoulder an affectionate stroke as he was reversing into the main channel of the canal. She then did the introductions.

"This is Anton, my favourite driver, and most trusted, and this is Steve, a friend of mine. He's English."

"Irish, actually," corrected Steve.

Claudia gave him a puzzled look. "We'll go into the cabin. Anton knows where we're headed."

"OK, after you." As she stooped under the small door Steve was able to admire at close quarters her light green trousers, which were beautifully cut and hugged her hips and thighs.

When they were both inside the cabin, Claudia took charge. "If you want a running commentary as we go down the Grand Canal I can do that for you. If not, we'll shut the curtains so there's no distractions and I'll tell you what Brosnich cleared me for about Sergio. By then we'll be there for lunch and then the rest of the afternoon could be free time."

Steve leaned back against the cushioned sides. "Yes," he said. "Shut the curtains, tell me where we're going and about Sergio and I'll try not to be too distracted."

She quickly drew the curtains on both sides and took the bench seat directly opposite him, smiling. There's the first distraction, thought Steve.

"Where are we headed?" he asked.

"Isola di San Clemente, roughly halfway between the Guidecca part of the city and the Lido. It's had a very chequered history – monastery, lunatic asylum and now, to quote its brochure, 'a five-star luxury resort for an elite tourist clientele'."

"Sounds just my sort of place," said Steve. "Now, give me the lowdown on Sergio and Brosnich."

"It's complicated," she said, stretching back so her head touched the curtained window. The second distraction, thought Steve, as he was now able to admire the short-sleeved white blouse she was wearing. He noted the faint light green pattern in it, the same green as her trousers. And as she stretched out he was able to fully appreciate her figure. 'Concentrate, Cromarty,' he said to himself.

She leaned forward. "It seems Brosnich had been aware of Sergio's military background and then his involvement in some sort of land-use surveillance for some time. Then, about five years ago, Sergio fed some classified AISI information to him and after making checks on him Brosnich introduced him to me and gave him some low-level work as a try-out. So for a few months we met fairly regularly, but away from Venice. Became quite friendly actually." Here she gave what Steve took as a rueful smile. "But I became concerned, because his conversations began to indicate an unhealthy interest or attitude towards his daughter. I think that may have been the reason why she never came back to Venice. I mentioned this in my report to Brosnich and a few weeks after that I was informed by him that the link had been cut. I didn't know until yesterday that it roughly coincided with Sergio trying to seek out some classified stuff from Brosnich, and that just wasn't on. So my meetings with him were stopped abruptly. And although I didn't know it at the time, I had a double security check put on me to make sure I hadn't been contaminated.

"Then a couple of years ago Brosnich got to know of Sergio's daughter doing voluntary work in Cameroon in a region bordering Northern Nigeria where Boko Haram were active. Sergio's name was then placed on a 'definite suspect' list. Brosnich told me that that information had been sent through to London."

Steve nodded. "His name being on the suspect list, yes, but I didn't know the background to it."

"Does that make a difference for you?" she asked.

"It might, I don't know. But there's another thing you might help us with."

"What's that?"

He passed across to her a copy of the message that he and Macbride had found in the cemetery that morning.

"Island drone," she read out to herself and then shook her head. "Drones I know about, but only what most people know. Island drones I've never heard of."

"OK, what about the rest?"

"Ionian Pride rings something of a bell," she answered, furrowing her brow in thought.

"Name of a ship?"

Claudia nodded. "Yes, but not one of the huge cruise liners. During the year some of the mega-rich cruise around the Med in their private vessels. To call them yachts is ridiculous. They're more like naval cruisers only they don't have guns, at least not visible on deck. They moor in the area alongside the Riva San Biagio. I think one of the Saudis has one with a name like that. Give me a moment, I'll check."

She opened the cabin door and called to Anton. Steve felt

the boat lose speed as Anton eased the throttle back and crouched down to listen. After a quick conversation in Italian she reappeared, closed the door and the boat picked up speed once more.

"Anton says there's one called the *Ionian Prince* that comes in once or twice a year and stays for a week or so. American owned, he thinks, not Saudis."

"And would you know if was due to be in Venice on the fourth of July? And the names of people who'd be on board?"

"All my clients come into Marco Polo or Treviso airport in their private jets, so I have nothing on private yachts, but given time I should be able to get hold of that information."

"How much time?"

"I'll make some calls at the hotel."

"And what about the second line?" asked Steve.

"That's easier," she said. "Fenice's the main theatre in the city and *Maria Stuarda* is an opera. Perhaps there's a performance of it on the fourth."

"You could find that out for me as well?"

"Sure. That will be no problem."

"Thanks. That'll give us food for thought."

"Talking of food, we're almost at the island and I've booked a table out in the grounds for twelve thirty."

"Impeccable timing, especially by a beautiful woman, always impresses me," said Steve, who was unable to prevent his deadpan expression from breaking out into a wide grin.

"I've heard of the wicked sense of humour of the Irish."

"And we can be wicked in more ways than one," he replied.

Claudia opened the doors of the cabin. "We're there, but

in light of your last remark I'll follow you out." She gave what Steve felt was an interesting smile.

* * *

The hotel and its grounds were all that wealthy visitors would expect. Claudia was well known to the staff and was obviously very comfortable there, while Steve had to make a conscious effort to appear relaxed.

"With today's weather we'll have a table in the grounds," she informed the liveried waiter.

Steve glanced around and was pleased to see there were one or two small groups already there for lunch and that tables and sun canopies were in place, so privacy was no problem.

"A superb place," he commented.

"Yes, but I have to keep reminding myself it's not for me," she replied. "But before we order, I'll make those phone calls. It might take a little time, unless I get lucky."

"I've got everything crossed," said Steve.

As it turned out, she was lucky; and she was back in a few moments.

The meal, largely ordered on a combination of recommendations from Claudia and the waiter, lived up to the surroundings. As they began to eat, Steve asked for more information about Sergio.

"I know about the tragic circumstances of his wife's death and not having a grave to visit," she said. "I don't think they were ever close and in any case he's not a grieving, religious type. But from the way he opened himself out to me I got the impression his relationship with his daughter, Maria, was not developing along normal lines and…" She stopped.

"And what?" Steve asked.

"The rest is supposition, not hard facts. But Brosnich is very good at making links." She raised her glass high, gave a wistful sigh and added, "and he's more often right than wrong."

Steve made no comment. He knew she had more to tell him.

"Brosnich has used all the US contacts in West Africa and no trace of Sergio's daughter has been found since the day of the raid by Boko Haram on the village in Cameroon where she had been working," she went on. "I think Sergio must have feared the worst. It was probably then that Brosnich realised that Sergio, as the surveillance man, could be a prime blackmail target for a terrorist group. When Sergio began to ask about work I might be doing, Brosnich had him put on the suspect list."

CHAPTER 20

Macbride had a good idea his call to Steve would spoil whatever he might have in mind for the afternoon, but he made no apologies for that. "Work calls," he began. "Familiarise yourself with the streets around the Fenice. I'm going to put Agnew in the picture; see you at Andrea's before ten tonight, I'll fill you in then. Make sure you can contact Claudia tomorrow if you haven't already blown your chances."

He ended the call without giving Steve time to make a response. His second call was to Agnew.

"Crucial news," he said. "We were too late to help Pinot."

"Not unexpected," answered Agnew, without a shred of emotion in his voice. "But I assume this call is too important for the mobile. As I'm already with Brosnich it'll save you time if we meet at the station at Treviso; you can get a direct train from Venice. I'll be there from three-thirty onwards in the Macdonalds café." He rang off.

Macbride was surprised to hear that Agnew was back in Italy, but he knew it wouldn't be just to collect Air Miles. There must be a good reason, but he was sure it wouldn't be half as important as what he had to tell him.

It was a short walk to the vaporetto stop at Riva di Biasio and then only one stop to Ferrovia. Although he had to wait half an hour for the next train to Treviso he arrived there before Agnew and was sitting having a coffee in the Macdonalds place when he saw him getting out of an expensive limousine at the station entrance.

"Travelling in style," commented Macbride by way of greeting.

"One of Brosnich's fleet," responded Agnew. He took a seat and ordered a coffee for himself and another for Macbride. "Your news?" he said.

"I'll give you a full blow by blow account of my chat with Parsons, but missing out the blows."

Agnew nodded. "I can imagine," he said. "Now tell me."

"Parsons had a real gambling habit, mainly involving the casino. Sergio, the suspect Sergio, also frequented the casino and latched onto this. Parsons got heavily into debt and Sergio helped him out, more and more. Eventually Sergio wanted some repayments, even though he knew Parsons couldn't raise any cash. It was at that point that Sergio suggested that Parsons should start to take advantage of the very lax system of checking the accounts of the Trade Links business. It started with relatively small amounts, but demands from Sergio increased and soon Parsons was dipping his hand into a very large till.

Pathetically, he told me he always intended to pay back the money when his luck turned. It never did. Over a period of about two years Sergio had Parsons well and truly hooked. He said he would help him to sort out his financial affairs and Parsons told him about his extra income from passing on messages from Pinot. Of course, that was of great interest to Sergio. He wanted to know more about Pinot, especially his address, which Parsons didn't know. However, he did tell him about his art store place, and we now know what resulted from that. About this time in our conversation Parsons was becoming more and more agitated and distressed. He started to ramble, and it was difficult to keep him focused. He mentioned Sergio becoming more and more concerned about the safety of his daughter and began talking of the need to do something to help her. Then Parsons began to wallow in self-pity and became more and more vague and incoherent. There was mention of the daughter being held by a terrorist group; he said Sergio was ready to do anything for her release, and he was desperate to prevent any knowledge of this getting out. At that point he almost passed out on me and I had to give him a good shaking. His final statement was that he thought Pinot knew, and Sergio would do anything to prevent him sending a message out to England. Then he really did pass out."

Agnew was silent for a moment or two before he spoke. "Things are fitting together," he said. "We can build on all of that. Thursday is the crucial day and it looks as though we'll be prepared."

"Thursday?" queried Macbride.

"The fourth of July, American Independence Day. That's why I'm here, to keep Brosnich company. When I told him of the first part of Pinot's message, even though it said 'No drone attack', because it was an American ship with influential Americans on board and the fourth of July was mentioned he couldn't afford to ignore it. By now, on his orders, the *Ionian Prince* will have left her moorings and be somewhere in the Adriatic."

"What about the second line of his message?" asked Macbride.

"That has to be ours. *Maria Stuarda* is not often performed, and on Thursday it will be attended by several British aristocracy. In all probability they will be walking the short distance from their hotel to the Fenice theatre."

"The walk could be cancelled," suggested Macbride.

"True, but if we and DIGOS can avoid doing that then that would be preferable." DIGOS was the Italian anti-terrorist squad.

"Cromarty should be walking round the area at this very moment," said Macbride.

"Keeping ahead of the game, that's good," said Agnew. "But we'll make a final decision on Thursday morning, in consultation with our Italian friends. Now I'll get back to Miramare and put Brosnich in the picture. We'll probably come down on Wednesday; a watching brief you might say."

Macbride checked his watch. "My train leaves in twenty minutes."

* * *

Claudia, though disappointed, understood that Steve's order from Macbride could not be ignored; she had been in similar situations herself. She gave him the directions to the Fenice area. An hour after leaving her, he was having a small beer in a bar just around the corner from the theatre entrance. Not for the first time, he cursed Macbride and wished he was spending the afternoon with Claudia. However, he wasn't, so he had to make the best of it on his own.

He checked his map for a reasonable wandering route, then left the bar, turned left to cross the Campo San Fantin, and walked over a bridge into the Calle delle Veste. Here there was a landing stage for those who wished to reach the theatre by gondola. Turning left again into the broader Calle Larga XXII Marzo, he was struck by the general air of affluence; many fine buildings, trendy designer boutiques selling expensive items, and a few discreet hotels whose frontages hinted at privacy, luxury and wealth.

He crossed another bridge, the second on his stroll, and smiled to himself; he had caught the Venetian habit of describing a route in the city by giving the number of bridges you would have to cross to reach your destination. He crossed the Campo San Moise, past the church of the same name, then turned into the Frezzeria, which had several expensive clothes shops. Perhaps it was as well Claudia wasn't with him; he might have been tempted to try and impress.

A further left turn and a third bridge and he could see ahead of him the Campo San Fantin, the starting point of his stroll. By now he was beginning to lose interest in this familiarisation exercise that Macbride had set him. He had noticed one or two apartments on his route that displayed 'SOLD' signs and he wondered what they would have cost to buy. A fortune and a half, no doubt.

A short distance further along, in the Calle del

Fruttarol, there was another property which appeared to have only recently been put on the market, as it bore a very new-looking For Sale sign. Steve was within twenty yards of its front door when it opened and a tall man with a military bearing stepped out: Sergio. Fortunately for Steve, he turned and strode off in the direction of the theatre. Steve had no wish for Sergio to see him, but the information that he had been there might be of use to Macbride tomorrow. To use his phrase, forewarned was forearmed. He made a further, more rapid, circuit of his route, then made his way back to his own place, feeling the afternoon had not been wasted after all.

* * *

At nine-thirty that evening Andrea welcomed Steve and advised him that his friend was just making his way off the Tre Archi bridge. "I think you'll enjoy your meal at an outside table tonight," he said to them both. "I don't think it will be possible for the next few days as the forecast isn't good."

"We'll take your advice," answered Macbride.

They ordered quickly, each keen to bring the other up to date with his day's work. Both were in an upbeat mood, particularly Macbride, when Steve told him of his sighting of Sergio near the Fenice.

"I'm going to call in to see him at his place of work in the morning. Forewarned is…"

"Forearmed," broke in Steve. Both men smiled.

"I think we're getting there Steve," said Macbride. "As long as our nerve holds."

"And our luck," added Steve.

"The Irish are renowned for having that in bucketfuls, aren't they? Now let's give our attention to this food."

CHAPTER 21

At nine-fifteen the next morning Macbride arrived at Sergio's office, which was in a block very close to the Rialto bridge. He hadn't formulated any particular reason for being there or any line of conversation. It would be a sort of social call, played by ear.

As it turned out he was only able to see Sergio's secretary. She informed him that from the previous Saturday he had taken a fortnight of his annual leave allowance. "He said he was flying out that night from Venice to Rome and then on to Lagos in West Africa. I do hope you haven't had a wasted journey."

"Don't worry, I'll see him when he gets back," answered Macbride.

Outside the office he turned right and made his way along the Riva del Vin. It was still too early for many tourists to be in the area. The second turning into the Calle del Cinque was empty and halfway along it he rang Agnew's mobile. It was answered immediately.

"I think you or Brosnich will be able to get this information quicker than me," said Macbride.

"Go on," said Agnew.

"Sergio was supposed to be on a flight last Saturday night from Venice to Rome. Was he?" asked Macbride.

"Brosnich is here, and he heard that. I'll ring you back."

Macbride strolled up the narrow street. There were several small restaurants, all of them closed. By lunchtime he reckoned the street would be alive with tourists and the restaurants would be very busy. He was almost back to the Grand Canal end when Agnew rang.

"He was booked to be on an Alitalia seven-thirty flight, hand luggage only, but he is listed as DNS."

"A ploy," said Macbride. "He's still in Venice and I don't know why. But up to no good I reckon. I might know more by midday."

"Keep me informed," said Agnew.

* * *

By now Macbride was convinced in his own mind that some sort of attack was being planned for the fourth of July, two days away, and that Sergio was involved in some way. On the assumption that two heads, or perhaps even three, were better than one, he rang Steve's mobile. "Any chance of you meeting Claudia this morning?"

"As it happens, yes. Despite you dragging me away from her charms after lunch yesterday she still agreed to see me today, but only to pass on any information she's managed to find out from her friends. She has a heart of gold, that girl. We're meeting at the artist's shop at eleven."

"Great," replied Macbride, "because I might have another little job for her." He cut the call, giving Steve no time to respond.

* * *

Steve was in the square where the artist had his shop at just before ten thirty, just in case Claudia arrived early. He ordered a coffee and sat at an outside table with a good view of the shop. He idly passed the time by watching a couple of stallholders putting out their stock of T-shirts, sun hats, baseball caps and plastic models of gondolas. They were looking to tempt tourists to buy, but while the older of the two seemed quite content with his display, the younger man was constantly altering the positions of his items. Steve wondered which of the two would have the greater success, but he couldn't wait to see; he couldn't afford to miss his meeting with Claudia. Much more would rest on that than the selling of tourist trade items.

He left his table when he saw Claudia stride purposefully down the Ruga San Giovanni and turn right towards the Rialto. She was wearing beautifully-cut cream linen trousers and a red short- sleeved silk blouse. She carried the same briefcase, and the briskness of her manner suggested business.

He hurried after her and the brief moment she spent looking in the artist's window allowed him to pass her, say a quiet "Buongiorno", and then continue into the alleyway which ran behind the shops. He stopped for a moment to consult his map and then turned to her as if she was a stranger and he wanted to ask for directions. She gave every impression that she was too busy to help and brushed away past him, but as she did so she murmured, "Pinot's church in ten minutes".

Steve was happy with that. He wandered back to the tourist stalls and spent time making his choice. He decided to favour the older man with his custom, and picked the most garish T-shirt in size XXL. "It's for a large Newfoundlander," he explained, as he handed over his money. "He'll be thrilled with it."

From there he walked into the Campo San Giacomo and crossed it to enter the church. Two elderly nuns were just leaving. He stepped aside for them and they nodded their appreciation and gave him warm smiles. He wondered how they would have reacted if they had known the reason for his use of the building.

Inside he had to wait a few minutes for his eyes to adjust to the dimness of the interior compared to the brightness outside. Claudia was sitting on one of the front chairs. He waited, listening carefully for any evidence that others were present. He assumed she had done the same, as she got up, walked up the furthest aisle and took a seat in a pew near the back. He walked round that way and saw that where she was now sitting was hidden from the main doorway by an internal stone pillar. He sat down beside her.

"You have the information we need?" he asked.

"Yes. The *Ionian Prince* left its moorings some time yesterday and it's now somewhere in the Adriatic."

"We were already aware of that," he said. Then,

realising how ungrateful his reply sounded, he added, "But thanks all the same."

"Probably what you don't know is that two of its passengers didn't leave with it – they're still in Venice. Harvey Mitchell, a US politician, and his wife. They stayed because they're both crazy about opera and they have tickets for the Fenice on the fourth."

"Hmm… do you know where they are staying?"

"As it was very short notice they're in a small hotel, but a very good one, in the Calle del Cristo. Italian security know that, but Brosnich is coming down to check that out, just in case. But that's not your concern, is it?"

"No. It's the make-up of the English party."

"I wasn't able to get any names except that I was told that the Royal Box was reserved solely for them on the fourth. Also, although it hasn't been officially announced, I know several press photographers have been quietly informed that they intend to walk from their hotel to the theatre. And security is to be stepped up that day."

"That will do us," said Steve. "Macbride phoned me less than half an hour ago. This is asking a lot, but it's very important."

"What is it?" she asked in a weary voice.

"We desperately need keys to get into the apartment which is for sale in the Calle del Fruttarol. And we need them like now."

Claudia pulled a face. "I'll try. Meet me near the apartment door at three. But I can't guarantee I'll have them – it'll take a big favour from a contact."

"I understand," said Steve.

She stood up to go. "Leave a few minutes after me. By

the way, what's in your bag?"

"An excruciating present for Macbride."

She shrugged and left the church.

* * *

Steve waited almost ten minutes before he followed Claudia out of the church. He made his way over the Rialto bridge and turned right for the line one vaporetto going in the direction of the Piazzale Roma. It was only three stops to the Marcuola, so he stood on the outside area of the boat, which enabled him to see the private jetty for the city's casino. It had been only a few nights before that Macbride and Sergio had spent time in there sussing each other out. A lot had happened since then.

From the vaporetto he walked past the side of the Marcuola church and along a narrow calle to join the main thoroughfare where Janice's bar was situated. Macbride was already there, seated at a shaded outside table with a glass of beer in front of him and a self-satisfied expression on his face. Steve pushed his bag across the table as he took a seat.

"What's that?" asked Macbride.

"I saw it and thought it was just your sort of thing."

Macbride pulled the shirt part-way out of the bag. "My favourite colour," he said, as he pushed it back into the bag and placed it on the chair beside him. "I'll treasure it."

"I thought you would," Steve replied. "Now how did you get on with Sergio?"

Macbride smiled. "I think we might have cracked it, Steve. He's taken two weeks' leave. He was booked to fly out of Venice last Saturday, but he didn't turn up. The flight left without him. That, plus what Parsons told us, and your sighting of Sergio at that apartment yesterday, tells me we need to have that apartment covered."

"What about the Italian squad?" asked Steve.

"They've combed the buildings on the whole route and there'll be a good ground presence. They are confident."

"But to be doubly sure, you're hoping Claudia can get the keys for us to get in there," said Steve.

"That's just about right, except to be even more than doubly sure, I want you to be in there tonight, and tomorrow I'll be outside, just in case."

"As my back-up," Steve replied sarcastically. "Out in the street and about twenty yards away."

"Well the way I see it, it's pointless us both having an uncomfortable night. In any case, one against one has never been a problem, unless age is beginning to catch up on you."

"OK. Claudia gets the keys, you get the gear, and..."

"We meet at the apartment at three. Almost two hours free time for you."

"Well I'm not going to waste any of it sitting here," said Steve.

Macbride raised a hand in acknowledgement as Steve got up to go. "I might even wear this tasteful shirt," he said, tapping the parcel.

Steve made his way across the Grand Canal and into the Rialto markets area. The Do Mori bar was his destination. It was almost full of workers from the nearby shops grabbing a quick sandwich and a glass of wine for lunch. He stood in a corner of the bar, ordered a glass of red wine and waited, making it last until the crowd thinned out.

The barman he had spoken to a few days before was washing glasses and generally tidying up the bar area. Steve mentioned that Sergio's group hadn't been among the customers who'd just left, and explained that he had hoped to have a word with him.

"They were here about an hour ago", the barman replied, "but you will not see Sergio this week. I heard him telling the others at the back end of last week that he was thinking of going off somewhere. I know he's very worried about his daughter; she's doing voluntary work in Nigeria near where those kidnappings took place."

"If I had a daughter I'd be worried too," said Steve.

They continued bemoaning the state of world affairs until Steve finished his drink and left the bar. Although he hadn't learned anything new, it had fitted in with what Macbride had obtained from Parsons and from Sergio's secretary.

At a few minutes before three, Steve was in the Fenice area. There were several groups of tourists, each with their respective group leaders, making their way towards the theatre for a guided tour. As Steve strolled down the Calle del Fruttarol he saw Macbride approaching from the opposite direction. They met and stood chatting. Macbride had a rucksack over his right shoulder. There was no sign of Claudia.

They continued talking for a short time, then turned and started to make their way back the way Macbride had come.

"This isn't promising," said Steve.

"Too right it isn't. We might have to find another way," answered Macbride.

Just then Claudia appeared from around the corner of

the next block of buildings. She joined them, linking her arm through Steve's. He gave her a quizzical look and she responded with a long face. "I couldn't get the keys to the outside door or the inner apartment door. I'm sorry."

"Blast," muttered Macbride. Claudia turned and frowned at him. "Sorry," he said. "I know you'll have done your best."

"But there's another possibility," she continued. "The block has a watergate onto the small canal at the back, with two doors leading into the inner courtyard. It's rarely, if ever, used these days and I've managed to get those keys."

"But we'll need a boat to access the first of those doors," said Steve.

"Yes, that's where I've come from. I knew you'd need one, so I got Anton to bring me that way just now. He's still there, down that very narrow calle, and he'll get you to the small private jetty."

"Someone told me you were a gem," said Macbride.

Claudia handed over the keys to Steve and Macbride passed him the rucksack.

"So I'll get into the inner courtyard, but is there any place I can hide for the night?" asked Steve.

"That's no problem," answered Claudia. "The main apartment door is up a flight of about ten or twelve stone steps from the inner courtyard. The area underneath them is usually used to store odds and ends, things that won't be damaged by water if we get *aqua alta* – these courtyards can sometimes flood a little. But that's only rarely."

"Should I have brought some waders, just in case?" said Steve flippantly.

"I think water is the last thing you need to worry about,"

said Macbride.

"Good luck," Claudia whispered. She kissed Steve lightly on the cheek before walking briskly back towards the theatre.

Macbride waited a few moments. "If I'm right, Steve, and Sergio does turn up to join you in there, do what's necessary. See you tomorrow." He strolled off in the opposite direction to that taken by Claudia.

CHAPTER 22

Steve walked quickly down the alleyway to find that, as Claudia had said, there was a launch waiting there. He doubted if it would normally use this canal, as there was little room for it to manoeuvre. The driver was Anton and, recognising Steve, he gave him a broad smile and spread out his arms. "No help needed. You know this craft," he called.

Steve returned the smile and jumped aboard.

"This will be the shortest trip I've ever made," said Anton. "No need to waste fuel." He began to use the poles of the adjoining jetties to steer the boat towards the watergate entrance that Steve needed. As soon as Steve had pulled himself up onto the jetty, Anton fired up his engine and the taxi slowly nosed its way around the block towards a larger canal. It was out of sight before Steve had sorted out the keys.

He unlocked the first watergate door, and was surprised at how insubstantial it was; it was made of thin timber panels and there were several holes near the bottom where the wood had rotted away. To Steve it looked as though high-water levels were not as infrequent as Claudia had suggested. The second door, which was at a slightly higher level, was a much stronger affair and had been recently given a coating of water-resistant paint. The lock too was a three lever, and although Steve was confident his picks would have coped with it, he was pleased he had the key so he didn't have to work on it.

He was keen to get in to the courtyard as quickly and quietly as possible and then to get himself settled in the area under the stone steps that Claudia had mentioned. Closing the door behind him, he crouched and listened. There was no sound. To his right on the opposite side from the steps and the main door of the apartment, there were four stained-glass windows which allowed a subdued light into the courtyard. He knew there would be a torch in his rucksack, but the light from the windows was just sufficient for him to reach the base of the steps and then move into the area beneath them.

Once there, he located his torch and began to take stock of his surroundings and the place where he would spend that night. There was a wooden stepladder, folded and lying on its side, two canvas director's chairs and four large paint tins with an old door balanced across them. On that was a rolled-up carpet, which Steve assumed was to keep it above the level of any encroaching water.

His first job was to change the position of the carpet slightly so he could squeeze behind it into the back of the area. This was the lowest part, but it was also the furthest away from anyone coming into the courtyard and making their way to the apartment.

He carefully took out the contents of the top half of the rucksack, confident that Macbride would not only have provided him with the essential equipment he would need but that it would have been packed in a particular order. Apart from the torch there was a groundsheet sleeping bag, black nylon tights, a thick, dark grey, woollen sweater, a black balaclava and black gloves. He put them all to one side and then, from the lower half, took out a supply of dried fruit, nuts, chocolate and three bottles of water. "I'll not starve," he muttered to himself.

Then he brought out a waxed canvas bag which contained the essentials for the job; a Glock 36 .45 handgun, a favourite of his due to its greater accuracy and stopping power than many heavier weapons. There was also the separate detachable silencer, and, in its leather sheath, a six-inch double-edged blade.

As he had no idea when Sergio might return to the apartment, Steve set to work immediately to make his preparations. Although the sleeping bag was of excellent quality, he reckoned the stone floor would be more comfortable with more padding under the bag. He partially unrolled the carpet and cut off two four-foot strips. These he placed on top of each other and then he put the sleeping bag on top in the furthest, narrowest part of his area. The food and water he put back in the rucksack and placed it within easy reach of the sleeping bag. Next he pulled on the tights and the sweater; the gloves and balaclava he'd make use of when any action appeared likely. Finally he checked the ammunition in the gun.

Satisfied that all was in order, he screwed the silencer onto the barrel and placed the gun under the balaclava and the gloves at the top end of his sleeping bag. Then he sat on one of the director's chairs and checked that he wasn't in the line of sight of anyone entering the courtyard. He was prepared. It was now simply a question of waiting and reacting to whatever he was faced with. He envisaged no great problems, as the element of surprise was his. Boredom could be the worst part.

And then he remembered something Macbride had mentioned. He pulled the rucksack across and felt into the small side pocket. Inside it was a small version of a Rubik's cube. Steve smiled. The man had a caring side after all. Steve had the mental resources to cope with boredom and discomfort, but he did find it galling to think that Macbride now had a free night to spend as he wished in a city so blessed with pleasurable delights. Attempting to master the Rubik's cube would be a poor second choice in anyone's book.

His thoughts were interrupted by the sound of a key being turned in the main outer door. He heard footsteps cross the courtyard and then climb the steps above him. The main door to the apartment opened and closed with a heavy, metallic clang as the bolts of the lock were turned. Sergio must have arrived to spend the night in the apartment before the final security precautions were put in place the day the British entourage were to walk near the apartment entrance on their way to the theatre.

* * *

A few hours after Sergio's arrival, Steve heard the rumble of distant thunder. It faded and then, at nine-thirty almost on the dot, it returned as a full-blown violent thunderstorm. It seemed almost directly overhead; lightning flashes lit up the courtyard and heavy rain peppered the panes.

Steve settled himself in his sleeping bag and began fiddling in a disinterested fashion with the Rubik's cube. In spite of the storm, he began to doze.

At four in the morning he was suddenly awake. He tensed, put his hand out for his gun and listened. A minute passed before he realised he had been wakened by silence; the storm had ended. He returned to his dozing state.

Upstairs, in the comfort of the apartment, Sergio slept soundly until he began to hear the seven o'clock bells of the nearby churches. He breakfasted well and turned on the television for the Rai Uno international news. No acts of terrorism were reported. 'It'll be different tonight,' he murmured to himself. 'They'll be full of it.'

He then checked once more the equipment he would need that afternoon; two grenades, the sawn-off shotgun and the black flag they had insisted he had to carry when he made the attack. He carefully fitted them back into the canvas bag, also black, in which he had brought them to the apartment the previous day. The shotgun was his weapon of choice; the grenades were a last resort if things didn't work out as he'd planned, and the flag was his guarantee that they would keep their side of the bargain and release Maria unharmed.

He once more ran over in his mind the timetable of the events. The opera was scheduled to begin at three forty-five.

He had already walked the route from the British party's hotel to the theatre and calculated that they would be passing the closest point to the apartment's main street entrance at ten minutes past three. At three o'clock he would be in the inner courtyard, waiting to hear the cheers of the spectators who would be applauding the party as they approached along the Calle della Fenice. He was ready.

While Sergio was sitting comfortably in the flat, confident in his planning, Steve was breakfasting on chocolate and dried fruit washed down with water and thinking back over similar situations he had found himself in. There was a major difference from those others, as Macbride had reminded him; for the first time, officially, the ultimate responsibility for action in this sort of situation rested on Steve's shoulders, although, as he well knew, questions would undoubtedly be asked.

The morning was as boring as Steve had thought it would be, but about lunchtime he became aware of the sound of softly-moving water. He cautiously looked round the edge of the carpet roll. Dim light from the windows shone on the surface of a thin sheet of water which stretched from the watergate door almost to the stone steps he was hiding under. The night's torrential rainfall had obviously contributed to an *aqua alta*. He hoped it had reached its limits now, as he had no wish to spend the remaining hours crouched up to his ankles in standing water.

Two hours later he heard the main apartment door being opened and then heavy footsteps coming down the steps above him; Sergio was on the move. Steve held his gun, crouched down, and didn't move a muscle. He was sure he couldn't be seen, but when Sergio began to pull the wooden stepladder out from beside the carpet, he was ready to move.

Sergio had no inkling that Steve was there. He got the ladder and carried it across towards the courtyard door, then opened it out. He returned to the apartment and a few minutes later came back with a large, black canvas bag, which was obviously heavy, and placed it on the topmost flat step of the ladder. Again he made his way back to the apartment, but there was no sound of any key being turned. From this Steve reckoned that Sergio was concerned that his important gear should be well out of reach of any water but also easy to hand. Not locking the apartment door would help to ensure quick and easy access to the courtyard. Finally, and crucially, preparing so early suggested that he was extremely nervous about the whole thing; he wanted it over and done with.

Steve simply waited; he was ready, but not anxious. At a quarter to three, he heard Sergio moving down the steps again. He pulled on his gloves and balaclava, picked up his gun with its silencer attached, then moved to one side of the rolled carpet. He watched Sergio, who, completely unaware of his presence, was beginning to unpack the contents of his bag.

He had carefully placed the shotgun on the second to top rung of the steps when Steve spoke. "There's no way that this will get them to release your daughter," he said.

Sergio spun round, looking uncertainly towards the watergate door. Steve had spoken so quietly that he could not be sure exactly where the voice had come from.

Steve moved out from his hiding place. "Believe me," he said. "They cannot be trusted."

Sergio faced Steve, with no more than five yards between them. More crucially, as far as Steve was concerned, Sergio was two yards from the shotgun on the wooden step.

"Maria is all I have left," said Sergio. "This is the only way." He was edging towards the shotgun. "And you are not going to stop me," he added, as he made a grab for the weapon.

It was a futile move. Steve's gun was already in his hand. He crouched and fired twice. The first shot hit Sergio in the chest, the second entered under his chin and exited through the top of his head. He folded back against the steps. The shotgun clattered down; Sergio was dead before his body crumpled onto the stone floor.

There was no need for Steve to check, but he picked up the shotgun and fired a single shot through the bottom panel of the inner watergate door, then placed the gun beside Sergio's body.

Five minutes later, after he had packed his gear back into the rucksack, he opened the main door from the inside and stepped out, to be met by a smiling Macbride.

"The weather caused a change of plan," said Macbride. "Both route and timing. But I assume it didn't affect you."

"Not in the slightest," replied Steve as he handed the rucksack back to Macbride. "But there's a body in there to be seen to."

"Agnew will see to that later," said Macbride. "At the moment he's with the opera party."

"Anything else I should know about?" asked Steve.

"Just bits and pieces. Oh, and Parsons has committed suicide."

CHAPTER 23

Macbride said he would phone Agnew on his mobile when he was sure the opera was finished. After that they walked briskly in silence to the bar near the second-hand bookshop owned by Alex. They ordered beers to be drunk at one of the inside tables. The waiter nodded his agreement. "The weather's not to be trusted at the moment," he said.

After the beers arrived and the waiter had returned to his position behind the bar, Macbride didn't beat about the bush.

"I heard three shots back there," he said.

Steve nodded. "Two of them were from my Glock."

"That's good, because Pottinger will go through your report with a fine-tooth comb."

Steve smiled. "I'd expect nothing less from him." Then, choosing his words carefully, he added, "In any case l can assure you that it will contain a great many accuracies."

It was Macbride's turn to smile. "He's on our side, but remember he has to convince his political masters that the new rules of responsibility are being followed. I'll have to bear that in mind too regarding Parsons' suicide."

"Very sad," said Steve drily. "Anything else I might be interested in?"

"The only other thing that happened while you were hiding yourself away was an explosion on one of the uninhabited islands in the lagoon. According to Agnew it was carried out by an Italian anti-terrorist squad acting on information received from an unnamed source. Evidently Brosnich was more than delighted; he reckoned it justified all his actions of the last few days."

"Well, the man has to appear to be earning his corn," replied Steve.

Macbride picked up his glass, then, without drinking, replaced it on the table. "Oh, I almost forgot," he said. "Claudia left a message for you. She's booked dinner for two at the San Clemente. Anton will pick you up at the Marcuola jetty at seven-thirty."

"An excellent end to an interesting day," was Steve's reply.

They both took long draughts of their beers, Steve thinking of the pleasing prospect ahead of him, while Macbride was teasingly holding back on the rest of her message.

"She did say something else," he said. "Now what was it? Oh yes, that she's arranged to spend the night in Venice. Would that make any sense to you?"

Steve smiled. There was no need to reply.

They finished their drinks before Macbride spoke again. "The two of us are booked to fly out from Marco Polo to London via Amsterdam tomorrow evening. Make sure you're there at seven."

"We're not required for any tidying up here?" asked Steve.

"No. Agnew will already be liaising with his Italian counterpart before he flies back to the UK tonight."

"And what about our reports?" asked Steve.

"To be with him by Friday. I'll check yours for any grammatical errors before I put them on his desk. Then the three of us will meet Pottinger in London for the debrief."

Steve nodded. "I'll see you at Marco Polo tomorrow. Now I'm going to have a quiet half on my own before I go back to my apartment and get spruced up ready for my date with Claudia."

Macbride took the hint and left. Steve checked his watch; he had an hour to spend to enjoy the tranquillity of the square with the soft shadows from the Miracoli church creeping over it. There was time to reflect on the events of the last two days. The violent death of Pinot had been sad and regrettable; the confrontation with Sergio and its successful conclusion had had an air of inevitability about it. This was the sort of world in which he had worked for twenty years. He wasn't completely inured to it – perhaps he never would be – but he knew that when Agnew or Macbride, or their successors, next called him he would be ready.

In the meantime, there was Claudia.